Adam of the Road

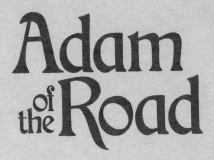

Adam of the Road

Elizabeth Janet Gray

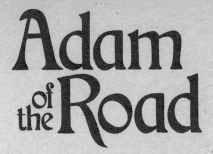

Cover Illustration by Neil Truscott
Inside Illustrations by Robert Lawson

SCHOLASTIC INC.
New York Toronto London Auckland Sydney

ISBN 0-590-33983-4

Copyright © 1942 by Elizabeth Gray and Robert Lawson, Copyright © renewed 1970 by Elizabeth Janet Gray and John Boyd, Executor of the Estate of Robert Lawson. All rights reserved. Published by Scholastic Inc., 730 Broadway, New York, NY 10003, by arrangement with The Viking Press, Inc.

23 22 21 20 19 18 17 16 15 14 13 12   3 4 5 6 7/9

Contents

Song

The road runs straight up hill and down,
Beyond the bridge and mill wheel brown,
Through field and forest, dale and town —
    But here stay I.

Wayfarers pass with never a care,
They walk or ride, or stand and stare,
Meeting, no doubt, adventurers rare —
    They pass me by.

Under the sky the birds fly free,
Squirrels and foxes have their glee,
Free as air is the humble bee —
    I can but sigh.

Matins to nones the bell goes Dong,
From nones again to evensong,
Latin and prayers the whole day long —
      I think I'll die.

I want to sing and jump and run,
Mile on mile in the wind and sun,
Sleep somewhere else when day is done —
      But here I lie.

The cuckoo now has changed his tune,
Each passing day leaves less of June,
Roger, sure, will be coming soon —
      Away we'll fly!

ENDED
OXFORD
APRIL, 1295

CHE—

EWELME

A MAP
of the
TRAVELS of
ADAM

MARTYR'S
WORTHY

ALTON

AIRESFORD

FOR—

WINCHESTER

ST. GILES'S
HILL

ITCHEN

TI—

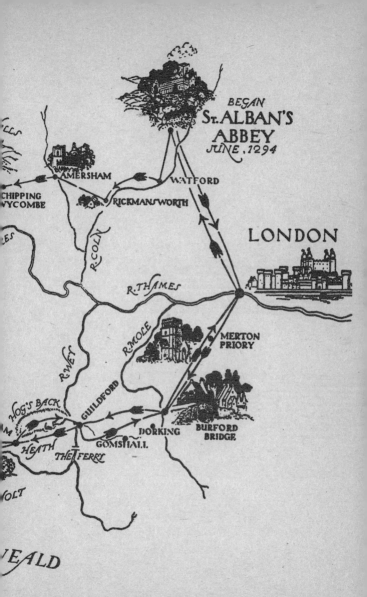

BEGAN
Sт. ALBAN'S
ABBEY
JUNE, 1294

WATFORD

AMERSHAM

CHIPPING
WYCOMBE

RICKMANSWORTH

R. COLN

R. THAMES

LONDON

R. WEY

R. MOLE

MERTON
PRIORY

HOG'S BACK

GUILDFORD

HEATH

THE FERRY

GOMSHALL

DORKING

BURFORD
BRIDGE

WEALD

Adam

AFTER a May as gray and cold as December, June came in, that year of 1294, sunny and warm and full of birds and blossoms and all the other happy things the songs praise May for. Adam Quartermayne, who had been looking for his father ever since Easter, thought that now he would surely come. Every morning when he rolled out of his bed in the long dormitory where the schoolboys slept, he said to himself, "Today he's coming! I know it!" and every night, disappointed but not daunted, he put himself to sleep making up stories about how his father would come next day.

Sometimes he made him come just at the end of choir practice, sometimes at the beginning of the lesson in grammar, sometimes in the middle of dinner when the boys ate their meat and pottage in silence while a master read aloud in Latin from the lives of the saints. However Adam's stories began, they all ended with Roger the minstrel taking Adam right out of school. Across the courtyard they would go striding, Adam with his own harp over his shoulder and his father's viol under his arm; through the gateway they would pass and over the river to the highway that led to London and all the wide, free world.

It was a famous school that the monks kept in the Abbey of St. Alban, but Adam had had enough of it. Five long months ago his father had left him there while he himself went to France, to the minstrels' school held during Lent each year at Cambrai, where he would learn new romances to tell to the lords and ladies of England.

Roger Quartermayne was no ordinary minstrel, picking up an uncertain penny telling rough yarns in innyards and marketplaces, filling in gaps in his memory with juggling and tumbling and piping as the poorer sort did. He could play the viol; he could chant long romances in French about King Alisaunder, or Charlemagne and his knights, or the British King Arthur and the search for the

Holy Grail. He was welcome at manor houses and at great feasts in castles, and everywhere people gave him rich gifts, a length of cloth for a surcoat, a purse full of silver pennies, or a gold clasp to fasten his mantle. He went attended by a boy to carry his viol and to sing with him when there were songs in the tales, or harp a little in the interludes, and that boy, from his eighth birthday till his eleventh last February, had been Roger's son Adam.

So Adam watched eagerly for his father and talked endlessly about him to the other boys in school. He always spoke of him as Roger the minstrel, as if everyone must have heard of him, and if he was a little cocky about being the son of such a man, they forgave him. They liked Adam, because he was tousle-headed and snub-nosed, wide-mouthed and square-jawed, because his gray eyes were honest and twinkling, because he sang so well and knew so many stories, and because, though he boasted about Roger, he had a humble enough opinion of himself. They watched for Roger too, and they all expected him, from Adam's description, to be as handsome as Earl Gilbert, who came sometimes to the abbey, but kinder, as brave as the king, but younger, and as grand as the abbot himself, but more comfortable.

Three things Adam had to comfort him while the good June days went slowly to waste: his harp, his friend Perkin, and his dog Nick.

His harp was the small harp of the time, which he carried slung by a thong over his shoulder. His father had taught him to play it when he was a very little boy, living up in the north in a stone house in the shadow of York Minster. Here at the abbey school he kept it on the shelf at the head of his bed. On rainy days when they had free times in the hall after the long hours of lessons, the boys would send him to get it, and he would pluck its strings and tell what he could remember of the tales he had heard from Roger the minstrel. At first the boys from the midlands made fun of his northern dialect, but he turned to French a few times and silenced them. Not many of these sons of franklins and burgesses knew the language of the court folk. Or he would sing the verses of a song they all knew and they would join in on the refrains. Sometimes they would make up more stanzas of their own.

The masters didn't like it very well, for the church officially disapproved of minstrels' tales. If they heard him they would stop him, or make him tell stories about the saints in-

stead; but oftener they just pretended not to hear him. His stories were about courtesy and chivalry, never the rude fabliaux making mock of holy things that the poorer sort of minstrel told.

Perkin, his friend, who slept in the cot next to his, was a thin, tall, dark-haired boy with a high nose and an intense, brooding look in his brown eyes. He looked a little like a hawk, except when he smiled; then his white teeth would flash and his whole face would light up. He was a year older than Adam, and a great deal farther on in learning. He was looking forward to going on to the university at Oxford. "I shall study the law," he whispered once to Adam, "and someday I'll be chief adviser to the king, like Walter Langton. He started a poor man. You will see."

Perkin's father was a plowman in Ewelme, and Perkin would have had to be a plowman too if it had not been for the parish priest. He first taught Perkin his letters and then persuaded his father to let him go on and take as much learning as he could hold; it would be a good deal, the priest thought. The plowman had to pay a fine to the lord of the manor to set his son free, and the parish priest had to persuade his brother, who was a monk at St. Alban's, to make some special efforts to get Perkin into the abbey school. Altogether, several people had been put to considerable trouble about Perkin's education, which made Perkin very serious — till Adam came.

Adam and Perkin had been fast friends since they first saw each other. The master had lifted Perkin by the belt from the table where he was bent over a parchment, and said (in Latin, for all their talk in school was in Latin, which was hard for Adam at first): "Here's a new boy. Show him around and see that he doesn't get into trouble." As it turned out, Adam soon got Perkin into trouble, through his dog Nick. Perkin hadn't minded. He was rather pleased, after having been so very good and serious for so long, to swagger a bit over his misdoings and show that he too could take a beating without flinching.

The dog Nick was a red spaniel with long silky ears and a tail that never stopped wagging so long as he was with Adam. He had followed at Adam's heels since he was a round, wriggling ball of a puppy, small enough to walk underneath the other dogs without stooping; he had slept with Adam — he was warm and soft to have in bed on cold nights — and had eaten some of whatever Adam had to eat; he was happy or tired or sad according as Adam was happy or tired

17

or sad; his brown eyes were constantly on Adam's face and he went to great lengths to please his young god and master. He even learned a few tricks to do for crowds in the marketplace or at the fair, though he was not one of those meager, scrounging, anxious, performing dogs any more than Roger was the wrong kind of minstrel.

More than once Adam and Perkin had smuggled Nick into school and tried to keep him hidden in their beds, but he would come out and wag his tail at the master, and he made so much trouble for them that in the end they had to give up the idea. An old woman across the river kept him, and Adam paid her out of the dwindling store of pennies that Roger had left him. Every saint's day and holiday he went to see Nick, to play with him and take him for walks over the fields.

If it had not been for his harp, and Perkin, and Nick, Adam could hardly have endured the long time of waiting for Roger to come back from France.

Nick

ADAM and Perkin were going to see Nick. Adam had saved him part of his meat from dinner and Perkin had saved him a hunk of bread. That was good of Perkin, for in spite of being so thin he was always hungrier than Adam and needed to eat more — and Nick wasn't his dog. Besides the food for Nick, which he carried in the leather wallet hung on his belt, Adam had his harp over his shoulder.

It was after dinner on St. Alban's Day, and the boys were free till suppertime. There was no reason why they should not have walked boldly out of the school building, across the court, and through the gate. The porter would not have stopped them today — indeed, with the court so full of people coming and going, the porter would scarcely have noticed the two boys — but they had their own way of doing it. Nick was a secret and they were not going to lead any spies straight to the place where he was kept. To confuse the enemy further, Adam went first and Perkin followed a few paces behind him. It was part of the proceedings that whatever Adam did Perkin must do too. If Adam chose to hop six times on his left foot, Perkin hopped too; if Adam jumped to touch a branch of a tree hanging over his head, so did Perkin. Adam usually went first, because the things that Perkin thought of doing were always the same, but Adam could think of new things.

So Adam came out of the school building a little ahead of Perkin, and at once the bright June sunshine and the crowd and the air of holiday-making excited him. He snatched off his round green cap, threw it up into the air, and caught it on his left heel kicked up behind. Perkin was wearing the linen coif tied under his chin that most men and boys wore; he had to untie it first, and when he threw it up into the air it went wide and landed in a little heap right on the head of the prior, who had just come out of the church. The prior was a very important person, second only to the abbot himself, and extremely dignified. Perkin gave a frightened squawk and dived behind a startled old man whose staff and bag and cloak showed that he was a pilgrim.

The prior brushed the coif off his head as if it had been a fly, and sailed on, his black robes billowing behind him. Adam picked it up and stuffed it down Perkin's neck. "Here, you ninny," he said, crowing with laughter, "hang on to it."

They went on side by side, Adam's arm affectionately over Perkin's shoulder, his tousled, sandy head close to Perkin's neat black one.

The Abbey of St. Alban was like a city in itself. Here in these vast, piled-up buildings nearly eight hundred monks prayed and worked and studied, and an army of lay brothers labored to make their holy life possible. Besides the houses that the monks needed there were the abbot's palace, where he entertained nobles and churchmen and sometimes the king himself, the guesthouse, where lesser folk might stay, the almonry where the poor were fed, and the school. Then there were all the stables and barns and granaries, the laundry and dairy and mill and smithy. Most important of all, towering up into the June sky, was the heart and center of it, the abbey church, whose bells rang seven different times every day for services of prayer and praise.

On this twenty-second of June, St. Alban's own day, the great abbey was seething with life and color. Pilgrims had come from all over England to worship at the golden shrine where the saint's bones were kept. Beggars gathered in hungry hordes for the extra dole the almoner would give out to celebrate the day. Townspeople and country folk came to see the procession led by the abbot wearing the wonderful embroidered robe that the third Henry had given to the abbey. Now that High Mass was over, people lingered in the church and outside in the court, seeing what was to be seen, and hearing and telling news.

Adam and Perkin skirted around the north side of the church and slipped into the herb garden. In one corner behind some clumps of tall lavender a monk was working. Adam squatted down and pulled Perkin down beside him. They crept on their hands and knees among the tangy, fragrant plants and wriggled through the hedge on the other side.

Beyond the herb garden were the vegetable gardens, with rows of green cabbages and leeks and peas and beans, and beyond them a bit of orchard and the fish pond. There they stopped a minute to look at the carp, and Perkin would have thrown some of Nick's bread to them, but Adam said, "No. Come on."

They had the abbey wall to climb next. "Give me a leg up," said Adam.

It was an old bit of wall down behind the big barn. Up Adam went, a toe here and a fingerhold there, the top of the wall on knees and elbows, and a scraped hand down to Perkin to help him up. A tuft of pink valerian growing out of a crevice nodded in the breeze and shed its fragrance. Adam sniffed. He loved all the warm, bright, sweet things of the earth; he hated being shut up inside stone walls with the smell of cold and damp and books and woolen robes. So now he sat on the top of the wall and sniffed and let the wind blow through his hair and crinkled his eyes against the sun, and thought of nothing at all, but felt blissful.

"What are we waiting for?" said Perkin, who was not one to waste time.

Down below them was the little river; between it and the wall was a strip of grass and a narrow path; a gnarled willow tree stood with its roots in the water and one branch pressed up against the wall. They swung themselves down by the tree and walked along the path to the bridge.

On the other side of the river was the mill and the Fighting Cocks Inn and the road that passed by Dame Malkin's cottage near St. Michael's Church. Because it was a holiday the mill was silent and the inn was noisy.

"There's a wrestling match going on!" cried Perkin. "Let's watch!"

"You can if you want," said Adam. "I'd rather go see Nick."

"Oh, I don't really want to," said Perkin hastily.

The road led past an old, old Roman town called Verulam. Nothing was left of it now but some crumbling walls and piles of stones with grass growing in the crevices. People had taken most of the old stones and bricks to make new houses. The tower of the abbey church was built of Roman bricks, and so was Dame Malkin's little cottage.

"When the Romans came," said Adam, "the people who'd always lived here before went under ground. They're there still. They're fairies now."

"Our parish priest says there aren't any fairies," objected Perkin.

"That's what Roger told me," said Adam with finality.

Dame Malkin was a widow who lived alone except for her cow and three sheep and seven hens and her big gray cat and Adam's dog Nick. Adam was always afraid that Nick would forget him between visits and learn to love the old woman best. He whistled as he came near the little thatched house under the big oak tree.

At once the door swung open, and out rushed a little red whirlwind with flopping ears, big fringy feet, and a frantic tail. Adam went down on his knees, Nick plunged into his arms and toppled him over, and they rolled in the daisies on the grass together. Nick's tongue was in Adam's ear, his feet on Adam's chest, and his silky hair in Adam's face, but only for a minute. Then Nick was off again. He bounced up against Perkin's shins, he ran round and round in great circles over grass and road, he yelped with joy, his long pink tongue hanging out the side of his mouth and his ears flapping together over the top of his head. There could be no doubt that Nick was glad to see Adam.

Dame Malkin had come to the door and

stood watching. She was a short, round-faced woman with merry blue eyes and red cheeks. She wore a blue homespun gown, and her white wimple and cap were clean for the holiday.

"Get up off the ground, boy," she called to Adam. "You'll roll on your harp and break it, and I've been waiting this long time for a tune. Come in, come in."

First Adam had to give Nick the meat he had saved. He made Nick work for it. The little dog had to walk on his hind legs, roll over, and play dead, and even when it was set before him, even though his brown eyes were all but melting with eagerness, he had to wait till Adam gave the signal before he could fall on it and gobble it.

"I'm not going to make him do all that for my bread," said Perkin.

"Yes, you are too," said Adam firmly. "He's a minstrel's dog and he has to learn to entertain people."

He took the bread out of his wallet and handed it to Perkin. He would have liked very much to give it to Nick himself, but of course it was Perkin's bread.

"Walk," said Perkin, and held up the hunk of bread.

Nick, however, recognized but one master. He stood on his hind legs, but instead of walking as requested he snatched the bread out of Perkin's hands and made off with it. When he was safely out of reach, he stopped and chewed with his head thrown back, and his eyes rolled at the boys till the whites showed. If either of them moved he picked up the rest of the bread and ran a little farther away before he stopped and chewed again. He was distinctly laughing at them.

"Come in, come in," said Dame Malkin. "Let him be, the scamp. It's St. Alban's Day."

So they went through the low door under the thatch into the little one-room house. It was dim inside, even though the wooden shutter at the window stood open and the sunshine came in and made a square patch on the hard earth floor. The rafters and the walls were dark with smoke, but otherwise everything was neat and clean. Dame Malkin's bed in the corner was spread with a blue coverlet, her table was scrubbed white, and her oak cupboard against the wall had been rubbed with beeswax till it gleamed. Adam and Perkin sat down on the bench and she brought out a cake made of white flour, and two earthenware cups of milk.

"Here," she said. "You two need fattening more than the spaniel does. Wet your jolly whistle and then you can sing to me."

Nick came padding in and lay down on Adam's feet. The gray cat stepped delicately through the window, gave Nick a look of disdain, and went to sharpen her claws on the leg of Dame Malkin's bed. Adam gulped his milk, ate his cake, and wiped his mouth with the back of his hand. Then he wiped his hand on Nick's silky sides, and took his harp from his shoulder. He tightened the strings till they sounded right when he ran his fingers over them. Ripples of music followed his fingers. He wriggled a little with pleasure.

" 'Sumer is i-cumen in,' " he sang in his high, clear voice, " 'Loude sing cuckoo!' "

He had heard the first cuckoo on a cold wet day away back in April, and he had thought then that Roger would come any day. Now June was almost over; the cuckoo had changed his tune and soon would be flying away, and still Roger had not come.

> "Groweth seed and bloweth mead,
> And springeth the wude nu — "

Anything could happen to Roger, and

Adam would not know it. Kings and nobles had messengers to carry letters for them, but ordinary people got news slowly and by roundabout ways, if at all.

"'Sing cuckoo, sing cuckoo, nu!'" he finished, and even in his own ears his voice sounded plaintive.

"Give us something merrier," protested Dame Malkin. "You sound as doleful as a hen in the snow."

Adam could almost hear his father saying, "Remember, Adam, a minstrel sings what his listeners want to hear. It's not for him to ease his own sorrows or tell his own joys. He's to find out how his listeners are feeling and say it all for them."

So now he looked carefully at Dame Malkin and saw that she was feeling holiday-happy and wanted someone to joke with her and tease her a little. He grinned and plucked his harp again.

"'Herefore and therefore and therefore I came,'" he sang, "'And for to praise this pretty woman.'"

Dame Malkin pretended to be displeased, but her eyes laughed. She raised her hand as if to clout him over the head. He ducked, and went on pointedly.

"There were three angry, three angry
   there were,
   A wasp, a weasel, and a woman."

"Oh," broke in the dame, "you're as pert as a pie, and I thought you were pining away with wan hope. I've a mind not to tell you the news I have for you."

There was something in the song about a magpie too. Adam sang:

"There were three chattering, three
   chattering there were,
   A pie, a jay, and a woman."

He stopped abruptly. "What news?" he said.

She folded her arms and hugged herself. "Oh, I'm chattering, am I? Well, I don't know about telling any news. I don't know at all."

"Have you heard something about Roger the minstrel?"

"No, boy, not for certain sure, but it might be something. A messenger came through here yesterday with the badge of the de Lisles at his belt and a parchment in his hand for the Lord Abbot. I got it from William the neatherd, who got it from Walter at-the-well, who's own brother to Harry the porter at the abbey gate, that Sir Edmund de Lisle with his train will be lying at the abbey tonight or tomorrow night, and they say Sir Edmund has a new minstrel with him all hot from some minstrel's school in France."

Adam's gray eyes suddenly shone out as if candles had been lighted behind them. "He's coming!" he cried. "Roger's coming!"

Nick got up and put his paws on Adam's knee, his tail wagging so hard that his sides shook.

"Now there was no name mentioned," said the dame warningly.

"They don't have to say his name," said Adam proudly. "He's the only minstrel worth talking about. Where are they coming from?"

"From Colchester."

"Then they'll come in over the heath. Come on, Perkin, if we go up on the hill perhaps we can see them. Come on, we've got to hurry!"

"They may not come till tomorrow," protested Dame Malkin. "It may not be your Roger at all. I only told you to give you hope, not to set you by the ears this way."

Adam flung his arms around her neck and hugged her tight. After a little gasp of surprise, she hugged him back, aimed a kiss at his smooth, hard cheek but kissed the air instead, had better luck with a swift slap at his rear, and ran after him with his harp, which he had left on the table.

He slung it over his shoulders, and it banged against his ribs as he ran. Perkin came thudding along behind him puffing and blowing, and Nick raced in front with flapping ears. Adam now and then gave a leap. He felt as if he could run forever.

Roger

ALL the bells were ringing for evensong, the great bell of the abbey, the smaller bells of St. Peter's, the silvery bells of St. Michael's, and, distant and belated, the bells of St. Stephen's. Adam and Perkin, small and lonely figures on the high, empty heath, wondered what they ought to do.

"We don't want to miss supper," said Perkin.

"Look!" cried Adam.

Far down the wheel tracks that crossed the heath they saw somebody coming. Several times they had thought they saw travelers approaching, and each time they had turned out to be sheep, but these were unmistakable men on horseback. The breeze brought the faint jingling of the silver bells on their harnesses. Adam stood on a grassy hillock and watched them come nearer, his heart beating so hard that it echoed in his ears. Some knights came first.

"There's one of the Cliffords — checky gold and azure with a fesse gules," said Perkin, pointing to a shield painted with gold and blue checks and a wide red stripe across the center. Every boy tried to learn the arms of the different knights and prided himself on the number he could recognize. Perkin knew more than any of the boys at St. Alban's, partly because he had a good memory, and partly because he took a lot of trouble over anything that he thought might help him to get on in the world.

"It's the de Lisle leopard I'm looking for," said Adam.

"Gules a leopard silver crowned gold," said Perkin, showing off. The heraldic terms were almost another language.

"There it is!"

A knight rode past with the silver leopard on the red ground blazoned on his shield and on the trappings of his great war horse. His helm was hanging down his back and his hair, which curled across his forehead and hung nearly to his shoulders, was fiery red in the sunshine. As he passed the boys he turned and said something to the man beside him. Adam was sure he had noticed Nick and was saying what a fine dog he was.

"My faith!" exclaimed Perkin. "They've got a carriage!"

Adam had heard that some of the great nobles had carriages for their ladies to travel in, but he had never seen one before. It was a huge affair, and it made a good deal of noise as it came lurching and jolting along the road. It took four horses to pull it and two men to drive, one man riding astride the first horse and the other sitting up in front of the carriage. It had four wheels studded with nails to grip the muddy roads; they were as big and heavy as cartwheels, but the spokes were all beautifully carved. The carriage itself was shaped like an enormous sausage, all painted and gilded, with little square windows in the sides and a door at the back.

While Adam and Perkin stood and gaped at it, the embroidered curtains in one of the windows parted, and a little girl looked out.

She had a pointed face with shining brown eyes and red lips. She wore a red ribbon around her brown curls, and a red dress. She was pretty.

Adam quickly commanded Nick to "Walk!" and the little girl laughed. That so much pleased Adam that he handed his harp to Perkin, and stood on his head until the blood began to pound in his face and his feet wobbled. When he turned himself right side up again, the carriage was past and the curtain covered the window. Adam felt a little silly. He had almost forgotten for a moment that he was looking for Roger.

Four more men passed in a bunch, and then a man came riding alone.

Adam really saw the horse first. It was a beautiful dappled gray, tall and strong enough to carry a knight in full armor into battle. The man who rode him was not a knight. He wore a bright surcoat striped in blue and green and tawny, and cut in points around the hem, and he carried a viol slung over his shoulder. His brown hair was cut short, his tanned face was square at the chin, and the eyes set deep under the boxlike brow were gray and keen and humorous.

"Roger!" shouted Adam. "Roger!"

The man reined in the big horse. "How, boy! Why, grant mercy, it's Adam!"

He flung his leg over the horse's broad back and the next second was standing on the heath. Perkin jumped forward and took the horse's bridle.

Adam flung himself on Roger. After a tight hug Roger took him by the shoulders and held him off to look at him.

"You've grown," said Roger. "You're whey-faced. Your freckles are all bleached away. I wouldn't give a pulled hen for those clothes they've dressed you in. But I've seen no sight in France or England that I liked half so well." He pulled the boy close and bent down — he was tall — to kiss him on both cheeks.

"Where have you been all this time?" said Adam. "Where did you get the horse? This is my friend Perkin. Nick can roll over and play dead. Look, Roger. Roger, watch."

But Nick was bouncing up and down trying to get at Roger's face to lick it, and Roger was patting him with one hand and stretching the other out to Perkin.

"I've been at a knight-dubbing near Colchester," said Roger. "Three days of jousting and feasting and tales. The new romances that I brought back from France went well — and Sir Edmund was generous. The horse's name is Bayard."

If anything could have made Roger more wonderful in Adam's eyes, it was to have a magnificent war horse named Bayard. Adam reached up and stroked Bayard's nose, which felt smooth and warm and hard under his hand. The great red-lined nostrils flared out and the big lips moved as if he expected to be given some tidbit to eat. Adam looked about and found him a tuft of tender grass, and he chewed it with a wide rotary motion till his bit was flecked with green foam. When he tossed his head, his mane swung and his harness jingled.

They were alone on the heath now. The last of the de Lisle train, the packhorses and carts, had disappeared into the town, whose clustered roofs and great tower stood out dark against the setting sun.

"Have they been good to you over yonder?" said Roger.

As he spoke he began to move slowly toward St. Alban's, leading Bayard by the bridle. Adam walked beside him and Perkin marched along silently on the other side of Adam, his lean, hawklike face alight with pleasure. Nick ranged ahead, nose to the ground, hunting for rabbits.

"Are you going to take me away with you?" Adam answered Roger's question with another question.

"Certainly, unless you'd rather stay here."

Adam's heart leaped with joy. "They've been very good to me," he said earnestly. "There was plenty to eat and I had a bed to myself, and they taught me to sing Latin hymns, and I learned stories about the saints that might be useful, but I don't want to stay here. I'm a minstrel, not a clerk. And anyhow, I want to go with you."

"I'm Sir Edmund's man now," said Roger. "We go where he goes. Tomorrow we go with him to London."

Tomorrow! Adam thrust his harp at Perkin again and turned five cartwheels without stopping. When he came up standing he had thought of something; he had remembered Perkin. It was wonderful to be going away with Roger, but he would have to leave Perkin behind. He took his harp back again with a sober face and threw his arm over Perkin's shoulders as he had done so many times these last five months. "I wish you could come too," he said. "I *wish* you could."

"It's a pity there's nothing in this world that's *all* good," said Roger, and added philosophically, "but then nothing is all bad either."

Perkin spoke for the first time since Roger had come. "We'll see each other again," he said. "Minstrels get about, and so do students."

Adam drew a long sigh, not comforted. He loved Perkin.

The Road

ADAM was too excited to sleep much that night. He heard the monks singing matins in the church at midnight and later a rooster crowing; he saw the first gray light of dawn streak the bits of sky that showed through the pointed windows.

He was up before the other boys in the dormitory stirred, and ran, shivering in the early chill, to the big stone basin in the lavabo to wash. He had new clothes from the skin out, which his father had brought him from France. He put them on carefully in the dark, the breeches, the long hose and pointed shoes, the sleeved undergarment called a cotte, and over that a sleeveless surcoat exactly like Roger's, made of a fine silk material called raye. It had blue and green and tawny stripes going round him, and the hem was cut with points that fluttered round his knees when he moved. He felt very proud in it, and wished that he had a looking glass like a fine lady's to see himself. On his head, over his cap, he wore a green hood with a little cape over his shoulders.

The room was getting lighter now and the sleeping boys around him were stirring a little. He turned all the things out of his wallet and counted them over: two silver pennies, the case containing his knife of Sheffield steel and his silver spoon, his comb, and some comfits that Roger had given him wrapped up in a piece of cloth. He bit off the end of one, and found it sweet and spicy. He selected half of them, the pink, the green, the brown, and the creamy one, for Perkin, and laid them on his shelf. Then he fastened the wallet and hung it on his belt.

He folded his woolen coverlet into a square and tied up in it his other cotte and breeches. The drab homespun surcoat which his father had said he wouldn't give a pulled hen for, Adam decided to leave behind, to be passed on to some other boy who needed it. He took his harp down from the shelf and hung it over his shoulder.

For some time birds here and there had been giving little chirps and chuckles; now they suddenly all burst into a joyful shout together. Clear pale light washed into the long room, and colors began to show: a green branch outside one window, the rose and blue designs painted on the walls, the bright orange coverlet on a bed.

Perkin rolled over and sat up and blinked. "If you ever get to Ewelme in Oxfordshire," he said, "my father is a plowman there. His name is Wat and he lives near the church. My mother makes the best kidney pie you ever ate." He paused to yawn and rub his eyes. "If you see the parson tell him I'm studying hard. He arranged for me to come here."

"I might get back here before I get to Ewelme," said Adam. "Roger says Sir Edmund has a great many manors and he's always moving about from one to another."

A bell clanged with a hearty cheerful sound, and at once the dormitory was full of arms and legs as twenty boys jumped or rolled or were dragged out of bed.

"My faith," said Perkin, "I better hurry."

That was all the good-bye they had. With the bell the day began. It swept them swiftly along, and apart.

For the last time Adam went with the other boys to the abbey church for the service called prime. After it was over Adam went to look for his father in the great stable. He found Bayard saddled and bridled, and Roger repacking the portmanteau which he carried strapped behind his saddle.

"Run get your things," he said when he saw Adam. "I'll put them in this."

Adam ran, and was soon back. He didn't want to miss a minute of this huge, dim stable, which was full of the warm smell of horses and the rich sounds of whinnyings and neighings and jinglings of harness and the voices of the de Lisle servants. Here and there a shaft of sunlight came through a slit in the wall, and motes danced in it so thickly that it looked like golden rain.

"Now," said Roger, fastening the last strap, "let's see if this will do. Up you go."

He had fastened the bag with all their possessions in it behind the saddle and covered it with Adam's folded blanket. Adam put his foot in his father's hand and swung

45

up onto his improvised seat. Bayard's back was broad and high, and Adam felt as if he were on top of the world. The bag was comfortable to ride on, and he could hold on to Roger or the high back of the saddle to steady himself.

"I can carry Nick if he gets tired running, can't I?" he asked a little anxiously.

"We'll see."

"Shall I go get Nick now?"

Nick was pretty good at heeling, but Adam had always kept him on a leash in a crowd. Would he know to follow Bayard? Adam wanted to explain the new way of traveling to him.

"Cut along. Wait for me beside the road in front of Dame Malkin's."

Adam slid down and dashed out into the sunshine again.

In front of the abbot's palace the carriage was standing, bright with its gay colors. Adam could not resist the temptation to go over and look at it. The door at the back stood open, and nobody was about except two men who were busy with the horses and did not seem to be noticing him. He climbed up and peered in through the door.

He had time only for a swift impression

of rich tapestries and cushions before two children jumped up from one of the benches and came to the door. One of them was the little girl he had seen yesterday; the other was a boy of his own size, evidently a page. Adam dropped back on the ground again.

"Look, Hugh," cried the little girl in French, "it's the boy I told you about. The one that stands on his head."

So she had seen him before she pulled the curtain! Adam wagged his head a little and grinned.

The boy called Hugh jumped down beside him. He was a proud-looking boy with curly yellow hair and blue eyes like bits of glass and a thin nose that seemed to be pulling his short lip up over his front teeth. He was wearing a sky-blue surcoat with wide sleeves edged with fur. He and Adam looked at each other, and neither one liked what he saw.

"He's got a red spaniel that walks on its hind legs," said the girl. "It's a darling dog."

She looked, Adam thought, too beautiful and highborn for words, standing there in her scarlet gown with the breeze stirring her curls and her brown eyes shining. Adam's heart softened and spread like butter in the sun.

"I saw the dog," said Hugh loftily. "It's a

good enough dog for a common tumbler, but nothing to any one of a dozen dogs we have at home."

If he had said Nick was nothing to his own special dog, Adam would have understood and forgiven him, but to say Nick was nothing to a dozen assorted dogs, that was too much. Adam thought longingly of wrestling with Hugh, of rolling him over in the mud and mussing up his pretty blue surcoat, but he had been too well trained by Roger to attempt anything of the kind. Minstrels did not fight with their audiences. He turned to the girl instead, and grinned.

"It's easy enough," he said, also in French, "to boast about dogs that aren't here to be seen." It occurred to him that Hugh had also said something uncomplimentary about him. He took that up next. "As for me," he said with dignity, "I am not a tumbler. I am Roger the minstrel's son."

The girl gave him a friendly smile. "Oh, I like Roger! Where's your dog now, Roger-the-minstrel's-son?"

"He's at Dame Malkin's. I was just going to get him. My name's Adam."

"Well, you'd better go along then," said Hugh sulkily.

It was good advice, but Adam was of no

mind to take it from Hugh. He pretended not to hear it. "That's the best carriage I ever saw," he said to the girl.

She made a little face. "You wouldn't think so if you had to ride in it. It bumps and jolts so that we're all bruised from being banged about from one side to the other. Father thinks it's wonderful, but I notice he never rides in it himself."

Hugh got into the carriage again and tried to pull her away from the door. "Come, Margery, don't talk so much."

"Well," said Adam, "I'd better be going." He put on his best son-of-Roger manner. "Farewell, lady, have good day." And added impudently to Hugh, "Farewell, Sir Honeycomb."

Margery, he thought, as he walked briskly away without looking back, Margery de Lisle. Now that was the kind of girl he liked.

After stopping at the gatehouse to say good-bye to the porter, he ran down the hill to the river and across the bridge. The morning mist was still rising in the wet lowland, and the Saint Mary's lace by the roadside was hung with tiny drops. He found Dame Malkin with her skirts pinned up and wooden clogs on her feet, out feeding her hens, while Nick, forbidden to come nearer lest he

49

frighten the fowls, sat on the doorstep and yawned.

Adam sat down beside him and told him about Bayard and how he was to follow close behind but not close enough to get in the way of the horse's heels. He was quite sure that Nick, though he might not understand every word, grasped the general idea.

"Well, I'll miss you both," said Dame Malkin, standing with her hands on her broad hips looking down at them.

Adam gave her two of his remaining comfits — a poor widow in a village wouldn't taste such sweetmeats once in a year's time — and a silver penny. She gave him a cabbage leaf full of strawberries that she had found for him. It was easier to say good-bye when you had something to give.

Already the first riders of the de Lisle train were passing the cottage. "Watch for a dappled gray war horse," said Adam to Dame Malkin. "That will be Bayard."

The dame laughed. "How would a minstrel come by a war horse?" she said. "I'll bet you your Bayard's no more than a hobby horse."

Adam knew she was teasing him. "You wait and see," he said calmly.

By the time he had finished his strawberries Roger was there, and Dame Malkin had to admit that Bayard was certainly a war horse. Roger reached down a strong hand to Adam and Adam scrambled up to his portmanteau perch. Out on the road it felt higher and grander than ever. He waved to Dame Malkin, and she threw him a kiss.

"Come on, Nick," he called. "Come on, fellow."

For the first few miles he was so busy getting accustomed to the motion of the horse and hallooing to Nick to come on or to come back, that he did not notice the road or the other people on it. He missed the last view of the abbey riding on its hill beyond the river, he scarcely saw St. Stephen's Church or the roofs of Sopwell Nunnery among the trees. He even forgot about the carriage and Margery de Lisle and Hugh. The open fields passed, and they moved into a forest thick with beech and oak and elm and fringed at the edge with ferns.

"Nick!" called Adam, seeing Nick about to dash into the wood. "Here, Nick! Here!"

"I see the abbot hasn't got his woods cut back a bowshot from each side of the road yet," observed Roger.

"No, Nick, no! Leave the rabbit alone!" shouted Adam.

"But they say," went on Roger, "he keeps

a company of armed men guarding this road all the way to London, to protect travelers from robbers."

"Here, Nick, come out of there! Nick!"

"Adam, stop screeching in my ears. Nick will be all right. Suppose you say nothing at all till I give you leave to speak. Let me hear the jays and ring doves instead."

Adam clamped his lips firmly together. For a while he kept turning his head and twisting around to watch Nick, but presently he realized that the dog was learning to follow. After his first energy wore off he stopped making side trips and investigations and trotted steadily along the road just a little behind Bayard's heels.

When they came to a brook, Roger stopped to let both Bayard and Nick drink. He flicked Adam's turned-up nose lightly with his forefinger. "You may talk now," he said.

"My faith," said Adam, "look at the road."

It stretched ahead of them across a long, level field and up a hill so far away that the men and horses on it looked like chessmen. For the first time since they had started, Adam really knew that he was sitting behind Roger on a great war horse, with Nick at his heels and the world before him.

"The Romans made this road, hundreds and hundreds of years ago," said Roger. "It will be here hundreds and hundreds of years after we're gone." He turned in the saddle so that he could see his boy's face while he talked. Adam looked away from the road and into Roger's keen, kindly eyes so close to him.

"A road's a kind of holy thing," Roger went on. "That's why it's a good work to keep a road in repair, like giving alms to the poor or tending the sick. It's open to the sun and wind and rain. It brings all kinds of people and all parts of England together. And it's home to a minstrel, even though he may happen to be sleeping in a castle."

It was, somehow, a solemn moment. Four wild swans flew overhead just then, and made it so that Adam never forgot what Roger had said and how he looked when he said it.

Going to London

AFTER a while clouds slipped across the sky and chilly little gusts of wind turned up the undersides of leaves in the thickets. The hills flattened out, and field followed wood and wood followed field in monotonous succession. Adam began to feel tired, and he was worried about Nick, who was keeping up, to be sure, but evidently with difficulty, for his head hung so low that his ears almost dragged on the ground. Adam was about to ask Roger if they could stop and rest, when Hugh came riding up on a somewhat small and scraggy horse which he rode with a condescending air.

"Ho, minstrel!" said Hugh in a bossy tone. "My lady Richenda wants you."

He paid no more attention to Adam than if he had been a fly, but spurred his horse and went dashing on to catch up to a group of squires ahead. Roger wheeled Bayard about and Adam called to Nick, and they went back to find the carriage. Adam forgot his weariness and gave no thought at all to Hugh; this was the real business of their lives, his and Roger's. He fingered the thong that held his harp over his shoulder, and wondered what tale Roger would choose to tell.

As it turned out, Roger did not have a chance to choose. Lady Richenda wanted to hear the lay of Sir Orfeo. Roger rode close beside the window and raising his voice to make it heard above the rumbling of the carriage and the steady sound of the horses' hoofs, he began:

"Lays are woven of love and sorrow, of adventure and magic, a little truth, and a little laughter. Most of them come out of Brittany, and none the worse for that. Listen, ladies, and I will tell you the story of Sir Orfeo."

There was a stirring on the other side of the curtains and some urgent though muffled speech in which Adam thought he recognized Margery's voice. Lady Richenda interrupted Roger. "Let your boy and his dog ride in the carriage for a time," she said. "Young things get weary."

After a few moments of confusion, in which the carriage stopped and several people gave out contradictory directions and all changed their minds several times, Adam found himself sitting on a cushion on the floor at the back of the carriage, with Nick stretched out flat beside him, and Margery beaming down at him from the low chair on which she sat.

He blinked his eyes to make sure he was seeing what he thought he was, and looked around. The carriage was like a little room, full of color that was bright even in the dimness, and fragrant with some rare, spicy scent entirely different from the fresh odors of flowers and new-cut hay that Adam knew, but sweet. Besides Margery, there were in the carriage Lady Richenda, whom Adam knew at once because of her age and authority, and a young girl with red hair rippling about her shoulders like a cape, and a couple of women whom Adam did not notice particularly because there was not anything very much to notice about them. He took his harp in his hands and leaned back against the side of the carriage to rest his shoulders.

Margery giggled. "The horse is stamping on your head," she whispered. "Doesn't it hurt?"

He thought she was a little crazy, till he looked around and saw that he had rested his head against the tapestry just under the hoof of a very spirited charger.

"My head's hard," he answered. "Takes more than that to hurt me."

"Sh!" said one of the uninteresting women.

The window on the other side of the carriage was open, and through it Adam could see Roger's head and shoulders as clearly as if he were a picture in colored glass. He rode along slowly with his arm resting on the edge of the window and his face turned toward the people inside, so that his words might find their target; only now and then he paused to take a quick look at the road ahead.

"Sir Orfeo was a king of England," he was saying in French that rippled along in short rhymed lines. "He was a strong man, generous and brave. More than anything else, more than sport or warfare, he loved harping. Any minstrel who came to his court was sure of a joyful welcome."

Adam ran his fingers over the air above his harp strings without making a sound, and Margery clapped her hand over her mouth and laughed with her eyes.

"Orfeo himself, loving to play his harp, had put his wits to learning it till there wasn't a harper anywhere who could make such music as he could."

The carriage did lurch and jolt, as Margery had said; now and then Adam felt as if his backbone had gone through the top of his head, and once he hit his elbow a whack that brought the tears to his eyes. Still, it was a different kind of shaking up from what he had been getting on Bayard's back, and that was a relief. What was more important, Nick was getting the rest he needed; he lay stretched out flat on his side, sound asleep.

Roger's voice went on like music, rising and falling, growing stern when he spoke for the king, and tender when he spoke of Sir Orfeo's beautiful queen, Herodis, and sad when he told how she was taken away by the fairy people to their kingdom underground. He told how Sir Orfeo in grief left his kingdom and went into the forest with only his harp for a companion.

"And now he who had had a soft bed with purple coverlets slept on the hard ground with only leaves and grass to cover him, though the snow fell and the wind whistled. He who had had knights and ladies kneeling before him, now saw no friendly creature. Squirrels ran from him and snakes hissed as he passed."

All the ladies in the carriage were listening eagerly; Margery's red lips were parted and her brown eyes swam with tears.

Adam knew the story well, for he had often heard Roger tell it. His eyelids drooped. He forgot about Margery and thought Perkin was there beside him; then he forgot Perkin and thought of nothing at all.

An extra big bump woke him up again. He opened his eyes wide and looked around to see if anyone had noticed that he had been asleep. Apparently nobody had; all their faces were turned toward Roger, who had reached the point of the story where Sir Orfeo gets into the fairy king's palace in the guise of a poor harper and offers to play for him.

"He sat before the fairy king and touched the strings of his harp as only he knew how to do."

An idea struck Adam suddenly. He picked up his own harp and just as Roger said, "Such beautiful sounds he found there that all in the palace gathered round to listen, so merry and sweet was the melody," Adam plucked the strings of his harp.

But Adam had forgotten to tune his harp, and furthermore in his sleepiness and haste, his fingers were awkward. Five doleful sour notes fell from his harp strings. Everybody turned to look at him in amazement.

"The fairy king said to Sir Orfeo," Roger went on loudly, frowning at Adam and smiling at the ladies, " 'Minstrel, your music pleases me well. Ask for anything your heart desires, and I will give it to you.' "

Adam, with some dim, sleepy idea of retrieving himself, plucked his harp again. "Twink, twank, plunk, plonk," it said nasally, and disagreeably. Nick sat up and whined.

The young girl with the cascade of red hair cried: "I wouldn't give him the half of my kingdom for *that*!" and everybody burst out laughing. Even Roger.

Adam turned red from his collarbone clear up into the roots of his sandy hair. He felt hot and stiff with shame. He fastened his eyes on the floor and he could not have raised them to save his life. He clenched his hands into fists so tight that the skin went white over the knuckles and little cups showed at the wrists.

"Never mind," said a soft voice in his ear. "Don't feel so bad. I'll bet Sir Orfeo couldn't harp any better when he was a little boy than you do."

Margery meant to be kind but she might as well have rubbed salt in open wounds. For one thing, Adam didn't want anybody to notice that he felt bad; he wanted people to act as if he didn't exist and never had existed. For another, that really was not a fair sample of his harping; ask any boy at St. Alban's, ask Dame Malkin if it was. In the third place, he did not consider himself "a little boy."

He grunted uncivilly, "Oh, I don't care," and continued to look at the floor as intently as if he were counting the threads in the carpet. Gradually his cheeks cooled and he heard Roger's words going on with the story. Sir Orfeo had won back Dame Herodis from the fairy king and they were on their way to their city again. Adam lifted his eyes warily. Everybody was listening breathlessly to hear whether the steward would prove faithful to Sir Orfeo and nobody but Margery was paying a bit of attention to Adam.

"I'm going to walk for a while," he muttered, and before she could protest he swung his leg over the doorsill and dropped down into the road. Nick followed him with a scramble and a thump.

The sun had come out again and the air was sweet with honeysuckle. Overhead the branches of the trees met and spilled sunshine in patterns through their moving leaves. In spite of the discomfort in his mind, which scratched his soul as haircloth scratches the body, Adam was glad to be walking again. It was good to stretch his legs and feel the air on his face.

The distance between him and the carriage widened; it was going rather faster than he could walk, but he thought he could keep it in sight.

"You, boy," said a voice behind him. "I want to talk to you. What's your name?"

He turned. A young man with a squire's clothes and bearing was looking down at him from a beautiful little chestnut palfrey.

"Adam, fair sir," he replied promptly. "I'm Roger the minstrel's son."

"Adam. Well, Adam, I saw you let yourself out of the carriage. Was the Lady Emilie in there?" He held his horse to a walk, and he and Adam and Nick went on side by side.

"I don't know which one the Lady Emilie is," said Adam.

"She has the sunset in her hair and blue

veins at her wrist," explained the squire in a dreamy voice.

This was the kind of description Adam was used to meeting in Roger's romances, though he had never heard anyone speak like that in real life. It must be the girl with the red hair. "Yes, sir, she was," he answered promptly. "She was wearing a green gown made of that new stuff from Italy."

"Velvet. What was she doing?"

"She was listening to Roger's tale of Sir Orfeo." Adam's face clouded. "And she was laughing at me," he added glumly.

"By Saint Simon," said the young squire, who swore fashionably by his patron saint, "I'd give one of my hands to make her laugh — or at any rate smile. Why did she laugh at you?"

Adam hesitated. Then he told the story. He exaggerated it a little. He played the sour notes on his harp and he made them sound even worse than they really had. The young squire, who had been looking rather unhappy, threw back his head and shouted with laughter. Adam threw back his head too and laughed, strangely eased of his pain. For the first time in his life he had played the part of an oyster. He had taken the bit of grit that was scratching him and made something of it that was comfortable to him and pleasing to someone outside. He had made a valuable discovery, but he did not know it at the moment; he only knew that he felt happy again, and he wagged his head a little.

"See here, Adam, since you're by way of being a minstrel, do you know the song Roger was singing the other day, 'Come hither, love, to me'?"

Adam knew it very well. He sang it.

"That's it. That's the one. How does it go again?"

Adam tuned his harp carefully, and sang the song again, with accompaniment. The squire joined in. He had a fine, true voice; it was too bad that it wasn't gayer. Indeed, thought Adam, looking at his new friend's long shapely legs and straight back, his color, his clear profile, fine eyes, and thick brown hair, he was so handsome it was too bad that he wasn't happier.

He had a silver flute in his belt, and now he took it out and began to play. He dropped the reins on his horse's neck and the horse moved to the road's edge and began to crop grass. In the third line of the song the squire went wrong and Adam stopped him.

"No, it's like this." He sang it once, and the squire tried again. This time he got it right. Then they went through the whole thing once more, the squire with his flute and Adam singing and harping. So Roger, riding back, found them.

"That's a good boy you've got, Roger," cried the squire. "He's taught me the song as well as you could have."

"There's some can teach better than they can learn," said Roger dryly, and reached down and pulled Adam up to his perch. Adam wriggled till he was comfortable.

They rode on together, the squire and Roger, and the squire talked about his falcon and about his flute and about Bayard, whom he much admired, and never once mentioned Emilie. After a while, when there was a pause, Adam whispered in Roger's ear, "I didn't mean to spoil the lay," and Roger said out loud to Adam's embarrassment, "I didn't mind that so much as the way you rolled out of the carriage without even a 'Farewell' or a 'Have good day.' But never mind. Green apples ripen in time."

It was afternoon when they got their first view of London, with St. Paul's riding high on Ludgate Hill and church spires pricking the sky above the massed roofs and trees, and the silver Thames looping around the city. The de Lisles had their town house in the

Strand between London and Westminster. They were considered rather brave to go outside the walls of the city; only a few of the powerful bishops had inns there, and the Earl Gilbert of Lancaster — and his palace, which was called Savoy House — was well fortified. But Sir Edmund liked the airiness and freshness of his house in the green fields near St. Clement Danes. It had the advantages, he said, of both city and country.

There was immense bustle and excitement within the walls of de Lisle House when the lord and lady and all their followers got there. The squires and maids went running about with perfumed and steaming baths; the grooms and stablemen were busy watering and bedding the horses; the carters unloaded the goods they had carried over so many miles. One cart had panes of glass in it, packed with the greatest care in layers of straw. Not many people had glass in their windows, but Sir Edmund did, beautiful glass, some of it painted, and he carried it from one of his houses to another as he traveled about. Smoke rose from all the chimneys of the kitchen as preparations to feed this crowd of people mounted to their climax.

Adam and Roger and Nick had a swim

in the river, which made a wide bend just at the foot of the garden. The water felt soft and cool, and it was wonderful to look downstream to London behind its wall, and upstream to Westminster and the towers of the great abbey and the king's own palace. Adam felt as though all his powers of seeing and feeling and wondering had been stretched almost to the snapping point. When suppertime came, though he had never before eaten in such a vast and beautiful hall among so many fine folk, he could not stay awake to enjoy it. He could not even finish eating the good food that was given him, but crept away into a corner, where he curled up on the fresh rushes on the floor and went to sleep with his head pressed close against Nick.

A Blush of Boys

ADAM sat on the brick wall of the stable yard and pretended that he was not lonely. Here he was, he told himself, sitting in the sunshine with Nick beside him; Roger was in the house talking to Sir Edmund, and Bayard was in the stable. Why was his heart so heavy?

Well, he missed Perkin. That was a courtly sorrow. Roland longing for Oliver, Damon for Pythias, Horn for Athulf: History and romance were full of noble friends grieving because they were separated. Shouts and a burst of laughter from the alley behind him, which was used as a tiltyard, stung him to greater honesty with himself. Even if Perkin had been sitting right there on the wall beside him, still his heart would be heavy because behind and below in the tilt-yard was a band of boys his own age having a good time without him.

He had been here nearly three days now, and they paid no more attention to him than if he had been a fly. The first day he had walked up to them happily and expectantly, and they all, led by Hugh, immediately went somewhere else. The second day they were nowhere to be seen. Adam stayed with Roger most of the day, learning the singing parts of a new romance from France. Simon was with them for a little while, and that had been a great joy to Adam. This morning he had perched himself up on the wall with his back to the boys so that they could see him and call him if they wanted him. He had played his harp, and he had talked rather loudly to Nick, and then he had just sat. Never before had his friendly advances been turned down; never before had he, Roger the minstrel's son, been ignored. It made him feel very low in his mind.

Suddenly he thought of one of the famous Proverbs of Alfred.

> "If thou hast a sorrow,
>   Tell it not to thy foe,
>   But whisper it to thy saddle-bow
>   And ride forth singing."

He shook himself almost the way Nick did, and, thought being practically action with Adam, jumped down into the stable yard. A pretty sort of thing he'd been doing, he told himself, sitting up on the wall for all to see his loneliness, when Roger had said he could take Bayard out and give him some exercise!

Bayard was a war horse; he was big and broad and strong enough to carry a great weight of man and armor, but he was no fiery steed. He was well past his mettlesome youth, and Roger was satisfied for Adam to ride him.

Adam whistled as he set about saddling and bridling Bayard, and in his struggle with the harness, which was really too big and heavy for him to manage, he forgot about the other boys. A stableman came to his assistance finally and heaved the big saddle onto Bayard's broad back; he shortened the stirrups himself, and then mounted by climbing on the edge of the water trough. Just as he was turning around to ride out of the yard, Simon Talbot came through the door in the wall, with his lanneret on his fist.

Adam was pleased to know the word lanneret. Some words were like pets to him, and especially the new words that Simon was teaching him. A lanneret was the kind of falcon that a squire was permitted to own. A king had a gerfalcon, a lady — like Emilie — a merlin, and a yeoman a goshawk. Simon had taught Adam too the right words for flocks of different kinds of birds. If you saw, for instance, a number of swallows together, you spoke of a *flight* of swallows, but you said a *walk* of snipe, and a *gaggle* of geese.

Now Adam sat, all eyes and eagerness, on Bayard and waited for Simon to notice him. Of all the six or seven young squires who served Sir Edmund, Adam most loved and admired Simon.

"Ho, Rob!" called Simon. "Saddle Pommers for me." Pommers within the stable whinnied at the sound of his master's voice.

The squire stooped to pat Nick and then came over to Adam. He held up his right hand with the heavy leather glove that came nearly to his elbow; on it perched a small hawk with his hooded head hunched down into his feathers and his talons clasped around Simon's wrist. Little leather thongs called jesses were fastened to the bird's legs and passed between the fingers of Simon's hand. On each leg was a small bell.

"I'm going to Westminster," said Simon. "There's a fellow there who's going to let me have a pair of Milanese bells cheap."

"You've already got some bells," said Adam.

"I know, but they're not right. One ought to be a semitone higher than the other. Where are you going on your war horse?"

"Nowhere special," said Adam breathlessly. Perhaps, he thought, his heart leaping under the stripes of his surcoat, perhaps Simon would ask him to go to Westminster with him.

"There's a blush of boys out there in the tiltyard. A blush of boys, you remember what I told you? — and a what of girls?"

"A bevy of girls," answered Adam promptly.

"Right. Well, they're tilting at the quintain on foot because that sorry nag of Hugh's is lame. Now you've got a real war horse. I believe that if you were disposed to be generous with him, they'd be glad to see you."

Rob brought out Pommers all sleek and shining and prancing delicately, and Simon mounted and rode off. Adam turned Bayard and rode slowly out of the yard.

He knew that Roger would not mind if the boys rode Bayard, for they all rode as well as Adam did, and some rode better, but he did not know whether he himself was willing to lend his horse to that uppish fellow Hugh. He was quite sure that he did not want to offer Bayard to Hugh. Let him ask politely for it as a favor! Still undecided, he rode into the tiltyard.

Tiltyard was rather a fancy name for what was just part of a wide alley with a quintain halfway down its length. The quintain was a post with a battered old shield hanging on it. The idea was to strike the shield with a lance in such a way as to knock it to the ground. It was much more fun, of course, and much swifter, to ride at it on horseback than to run at it on foot.

Six boys were scattered up and down the alley: Hugh and his younger brothers, Godfrey and Ralph, who were nephews of Sir Edmund; William and Martin, the sons of the falconer; and Matthew, the bailiff's son. Adam tumbled himself down from Bayard and said offhandedly to Godfrey, who was shorter and blunter and much jollier-looking than Hugh, "Why don't you ride at the quintain? You can have Bayard, if you like."

Godfrey looked at him uncertainly for a moment, and then gave a shrill shout. "Hugh! Come here! Minstrel's son says we can ride Bayard!"

Hugh, who was halfway down the alley, turned and came back, carrying the blunt-ended ash-wood pole that they used for a lance. For the second time he and Adam looked squarely at each other.

Well, sir, Adam was saying within himself, I don't care so very much for you, but I like your crowd and I want to belong to it, I'll do my share and a bit over.

What Hugh was thinking behind those rather glittery blue eyes of his, Adam could not tell. Hugh's glance wavered first. He turned to Bayard, and Adam knew from the way he looked at the horse and touched him that Hugh loved Bayard almost as Adam himself loved Nick.

"He's getting old," said Hugh, "but he's a great horse still. He was in battle at Acre in the Holy Land. Uncle got him in exchange for a white Spanish jennet and then he was sorry afterward because he liked the jennet better, but I'd rather have Bayard any day."

He mounted nimbly and Ralph handed his lance up to him. Two of the boys ran to raise the shield higher on the post. Nobody questioned Hugh's right to the first turn.

Godfrey said to Adam, while Hugh was riding Bayard up and down to get the feel of him again, "Hugh thought maybe Uncle would give Bayard to him, but he didn't."

Then Adam understood why Hugh had been so disagreeable. Suppose somebody else had got Nick! "By Saint Simon," he said, copying Simon Talbot, "I'm sorry." Some other horse would have done as well for Roger; time was when they didn't have a horse at all.

Hugh rode twice at the quintain; the first time he missed, but the second time he sent the shield clattering to the ground. Then Godfrey had his turn, and Hugh, glowing, came to talk to Adam. He looked a different boy; all the ill humor seemed to have been shaken out of him.

"Will Roger let you have Bayard again?" he asked eagerly.

"I'm sure he will when I tell him — I mean you ride better than I do, so if he'd let me he'd let you."

Hugh watched Godfrey critically. "He'll miss. You'll see. He's good, but Bayard doesn't like him as well as he likes me. Bayard and I understand each other. At Ludlow we've got a real tiltyard, and the quintain isn't just a shield. It's a wooden Saracen on a pivot, with a sword in his hand. If you hit him in the middle of the forehead he falls over, but if you hit him anywhere else he swings around and whacks you in the back with his sword. By Saint Hugh, that's real tilting!"

Godfrey came back, and, declaring that Ralph, who was not yet ten, was too small, Hugh sent Martin off next, and then William. "Do you want a turn?" he thought at last to say to Adam.

"Hugh!" cried Godfrey reproachfully. "It's his horse!"

Hugh blushed. "Oh, well," he said, trying to cover his confusion. "Minstrels don't joust or ride in tournaments, or go to war."

"Taillefer did," said Adam stoutly. "He was the Conqueror's minstrel, but he was a warrior too. At the battle of Senlac he asked leave of William to begin the onset, and he rode before the whole army juggling with his sword and chanting the song of Roland. Then he rushed on the English and was killed."

So Adam had his turn. Before he went to St. Alban's he had had some practice here and there, mostly, it is true, one Easter in London; he had not done badly then. It gave him confidence to remember that. He cradled his lance in his arm and he spoke to Bayard. Nearer and nearer the shield they came. Adam gathered himself together and thrust — and the battered, dingy shield dropped to the ground and wobbled over onto its face. Trying not to grin too broadly, Adam rode back to the others. He could not keep his head from wagging a bit.

"Well done!" said Hugh, with respect in his voice. He had been kneeling on one knee and holding Nick's collar while Adam rode; now he stood up and said, dusting off his knee very briskly, "This is a good dog, Adam. He's got a fine ear-carriage and a straight back. We haven't any dogs at Ludlow any better than he is — at least, not any spaniels."

It was wonderful how much better that made Adam feel. After Matthew had had his first turn and Hugh his second, the shadow of the pear tree reached the wall and it was time to stop. Adam led Bayard back to the stable, and the others went off toward the house with their heads together. In a moment Godfrey left them and came running back to Adam.

"We've a sort of company, we six, when we're in London," he panted. "Hugh and I are knights, and Ralph's a squire, and Will and Matthew and Martin are yeomen, and Margery is our liege lady. We've never had a minstrel, but Hugh says we need one and we all think so. You could be Taillefer!"

After that they were together every minute that they could be. None of the seven went to school — Sir Edmund's three nephews considered learning only for milksops who were not fit to be knights or for poor boys whose sole hope of advancement was through the church — but they were all subject to instruction of one kind or another from grown-ups. Hugh and Godfrey and Ralph had a tutor who trained them in pursuits necessary for boys who looked forward to being knights: tilting and riding and sword-play and hawking and hunting. They had a great deal of tiresome practicing to do, the same exercises over and over again, with very little praise to sweeten it and even less sympathy when they got tired. The falconer's boys were often busy in the mews, where the moulting hawks were kept, and they had to learn how to make hoods and jesses out of skins and how to school the young hawks and to care for the ailing ones. Matthew, the bailiff's son, must struggle with figures and learn to cast accounts and to know what was expected of everybody in a large and complicated household like Sir Edmund's. As for Adam, he had his work too. The northern minstrels were famous for singing together, one in the bass and the other in the treble. Roger had brought home new songs from France which Adam must learn and they had many old ones to practice as well. Adam had his harping to work on too, and Roger taught him to do some new tumbling tricks and to juggle knives.

"It's not real minstrelsy, but it catches the crowd," said Roger. "Some people can't appreciate a good story well told, but they like to have a lithe young lad dazzle their slow eyes with tricks. You needn't use them unless you have to, but it's well to have a second string to your bow."

When they were free to be together, the seven boys had endless fun. They were tilting at the quintain, or diving and swimming in the river, or running footraces, or having wrestling matches. In the long twilights after supper they played games in the garden, and Margery and Emilie and some of the squires would join them. They played prisoners' base and hoop and hide and hoodman's blind and, when the girls insisted, London Bridge. Adam would play on his harp for that, and his voice soared high above the others in the singing.

"London Bridge is broken down,
    Dance over my Lady Lea.
London Bridge is broken down,
    With a gay lady."

The joke of it was, though the song was such an old one and the wooden London Bridge had fallen down more than a hundred years before and been built up in "stone so strong," it was likely to come true again. For years and years the old Queen Eleanor had collected fees from all who passed over it, and never spent a penny of them on repairs. Now the stones were worn into holes in some of the arches so that you could see the water rushing beneath.

"Build it up with silver and gold,
    Dance over my Lady Lea,
Build it up with silver and gold,
    With a fair lady,"

the ones inside the ring would sing, and those outside would answer,

"Silver and gold will be stolen away,
  Dance over my Lady Lea.
Silver and gold will be stolen away,
  With a gay lady!"

Adam would twang his harp and look across the beds of roses and gilliflowers and lillies to the river and London Bridge misty in the distance with a faint light or two in the windows of the houses on it. A bridge is a kind of sacred thing, he thought, as Roger said a road was. There was a chapel to St. Thomas of Canterbury in the middle of London Bridge, and St. Thomas was a great saint and his chapel was holy. Yet the old queen had not cared enough about the bridge to keep it safe, and boys and girls never gave it a thought when they sang joyfully.

"London Bridge is broken down,
  With a gay lady!"

Jankin

ONE afternoon in late July, Adam and Hugh and Martin, and Nick, of course, were lying stretched out in the sunlight on the wharf. They had been on the river in the little wherry that belonged to the house, and now they were resting and eating some walnuts that Hugh had got from Lady Richenda. They were pretty old and rancid now, but the boys were hungry. As they cracked the nuts between two stones, they talked about the squires and which would become a knight first. Each boy had his favorite. Hugh's was the squire of the stable, a breezy young man who shared his passion for horses and got him many a chance for a ride that he would not otherwise have had. Once he had taken Hugh to Smithfield Market when he went to buy a farm horse to bring supplies from the de Lisle manor to Essex.

Adam's hero was still and always Simon Talbot, who was the carving squire. When the big saddles of mutton or sides of beef, the roast swans and peacocks and geese were brought into the hall at dinner and placed on the high table before Sir Edmund, it was Simon who carved them and distributed the portions. He carved with great skill and always looked particularly splendid when he was doing it. Then Simon loved music too, and songs, and tales. Simon had a pen case of his own and he wrote long poems to Emilie on pieces of parchment which he kept under the straw in his bed, and now and then showed to Adam. He was always in hopes that Adam could help him fit a tune to them, but as Simon would not change a word he had written, and there was a limit to what Adam could do with a tune, they never had any great success.

"Simon is like the 'squire of low degree,' " said Adam. He quoted the opening words of the romance which Roger sometimes told, but never at de Lisle House:

"It was a squire of low degree,
Loved the king's daughter of Hungary.

"He loved her seven years before he told her of his love, and then he went away and fought in the wars for seven years to do her honor, and then —"

"Seven years!" interrupted Hugh. "What did the king's daughter do all that time?"

"She waited for him to come back."

"Emilie won't wait any seven years for Simon," said Hugh with conviction. "Even if she wanted to, Uncle wouldn't let her."

"Why not?"

"Why should he let her marry a poor squire when she could have a rich and powerful knight like Sir Gervase? Uncle hasn't any sons, and Emilie is his heir."

Adam had seen Sir Gervase de Warenne, who visited de Lisle House with six squires and a band of archers in attendance and set the whole place by the ears. He was a burly, red-faced man with a voice like a trumpet; he wore fine bright clothes and when he turned around his mantle swung out and swept everything off the table near it. "Maybe she'd rather marry Simon," said Adam.

"It doesn't matter what she'd rather do," said Hugh carelessly. "She's only a girl. She's got to do what she's told."

Adam found it all rather puzzling. Hugh and Godfrey and the rest pretended that Margery was their liege lady and set themselves to do their showiest feats of tilting and wrestling in her honor. The tales Roger told were full of the reverence and devotion that knights paid to fair ladies and the desperate dangers they met gladly in order to win a smile from the ladies or a favor to wear on their sleeves. But in real life, it seemed, a beautiful young lady like Emilie was only a girl and it did not matter what she wanted because she had to do what she was told. It was strange — and what was more, thought Adam, it was very hard on Simon.

He asked Roger about it that night when they went to bed on a bench in the hall.

In the daytime the hall was the center of all the life of the household. On the dais at one end was the high table where the de Lisles and their guests ate, with their falcons sitting on perches on the wall behind and their dogs lying on the floor at their feet. In the center of the hall was the hearth, where on cold days a fire was lighted. Down the length of the hall on either side of the hearth other tables made of wide oak boards on carved trestles were set up and here the lesser folk who belonged to the household sat. After meals the cloths were taken from the tables, the rich, colored undercloth and the fine white linen overcloth, the boards were stacked against the wall, the trestles and benches pushed back, and there was room for minstrelsy and dancing, for games of chess or of dice, for talk and laughter. The ladies would withdraw to the room called the solar, above, where they sat long hours over their embroidery, entertained by the gentlemen who came to gossip with them or by the tales that Roger told.

At night, on the benches against the wall, or even in the rushes on the floor, slept some of the men of the household. The porter slept there, for instance, and the clerk of the kitchen, an archer or two, and Roger and Adam and Nick.

Adam liked the great hall at night. The cool fresh air off the river came in through the open windows and cleared the lingering smoke away. On moonlight nights the moon shone in on the embroidered wall-hangings and woke faint colors in them. Adam felt safe with Roger close beside him and Nick pressing against him, and he slept deep with his coverlet over him and some rather musty cushions under him. Sometimes, of course, people snored, and that was less pleasant.

On this night, after everybody else had settled down into quiet lumps and mounds of darkness in the shadows, Adam whispered to Roger: "Is Emilie going to marry Sir Gervase?"

"How did you know? Is it common knowledge among the young fry?"

"I guessed from something Hugh said."

"Yes, she is," said Roger. "There will be a wedding soon, and a big day for minstrels it will be too. After that — " he stopped.

"After that — what?" Adam prompted him.

"After that you and I will go down the high road again."

"Why? Won't we be Sir Edmund's minstrels any more?"

"Yes, we shall be his minstrels still, but he'll not need us all the time. We'll come back to him for holidays, for Christmas and Easter and Whitsuntide, but the rest of the time we'll be off by ourselves. It's often done,"

Roger explained. "Not many great lords keep their minstrels with them all through the year."

Adam thought about that in silence. He remembered what Roger had said the day they had left St. Alban's. How long ago it seemed now! "The road is home to the minstrel, even though he may happen to be sleeping in a castle." He would miss Hugh and Margery and the others, as he missed Perkin, but he would see them again. So long as he had Roger and Nick, everything was all right.

He began to feel sleepy. Nick got up and stepped over Adam, planting one foot deep in his stomach and the other on his thigh; then he curled up in the little harbor behind Adam's bent knees, gave a sigh, and went to sleep again. Adam slept too.

The wedding took place in August. Never had Adam seen such crowds, so many great folk, so much good food, such gaiety, or such music and dancing.

First, there was the ceremony at the little church of St. Clement Danes just beyond the gates of de Lisle House. Part of the ceremony was performed outside at the church door, where the priest met them in his finest vestments with a wonderful embroidered stole about his neck, and part, inside the church. After it was over they all went back to de Lisle House, and the feast began.

Emilie and Sir Gervase sat under the canopy at the high table, with de Lisles and de Warennes in all their glory stretching to both sides of them, and Simon very pale and handsome standing before them and carving one magnificent roasted masterpiece after another. When Adam saw the roast peacock with his tail spread he could scarcely believe his eyes, but everybody else took it calmly. The other squires were acting as ushers and seating the guests, and Hugh and Godfrey and Ralph in new surcoats with their hair washed and curled were attending with silver basins and ewers and fine white towels for people to wash their hands.

Between courses the minstrels performed, not only Roger and Adam, but a host of other minstrels who had come from near and far, attracted to a feast like flies to honey. There were minstrels with viols and harps and flutes and trumpets, psalteries and mere tabors. Never had Adam heard such music. There was singing. Adam himself sang first with Roger and then alone, his voice soaring high and losing itself among the painted beams of the roof. The flushed company sat silent for a moment or two while he sang.

After dinner spiced wine was brought and comfits and ginger and nuts and fruit, and there was dancing.

For hours the merriment went on. Some danced. Some walked in the garden. Some listened to the minstrels. Roger told the tale that he had brought from France, of the lovers, Aucassin and Nicolette, and Adam sang with him in the parts that were meant to be sung. Afterward Margery came dancing up to Roger with a gold brooch in her hand.

"Emilie said that was the best tale she ever heard and told me to give you this," she said.

It was a gold brooch shaped like the quatrefoils they were building in the stone windows now. Roger pinned it at his throat, where it gleamed against the rich purple of his coat.

At sunset the guests began to go. The sun's rays lay slanting over fields and river, and gleamed on the towers in the city of London. By groups in their bright clothes the ladies and gentlemen were making their way across the fields and down the rutted roads toward their dwelling places, some on horseback, those who lived nearest on foot.

The steward summoned all the minstrels

to the small room off the hall where he did his business. They crowded together in the little space and he made them a speech.

"Sir Edmund ith well pleathed," he said with his affected lisp, "with your performanth. He desireth to reward you."

To each of them in turn he gave a purse, a small embroidered bag with a drawstring, heavy with silver pennies that clinked in an elegant way. Adam got one too, and he was proud enough to burst!

He watched the other minstrels as they received their gifts. He had never before seen so many of his craft together at one time. One was old and had lost most of his teeth; one was young and handsome and gay, but cruel-looking; one was tall and gaunt as a tree, but like a tree he was straight and strong too. One was a little, dark-haired man with sharp black eyes and a thin, vivid face. His name was Jankin, and Adam liked him because he had smiled at Nick and leaned down to scratch behind his ears. There was one woman among the minstrels, Matill' Makejoye. She was a rough, kindly sort of person who could dance on her hands better than she could tell a tale.

Some of the minstrels went off at once toward London, some lingered in groups talking about places they had seen and people they knew, and some gathered in a ring to throw dice, ready to risk the pennies they had just received. The dicebox, it was said everywhere, was the ruin of the minstrel.

Those minstrels stayed all night. The last thing Adam heard before he went to sleep and the first when he woke up next morning was the rattle of the dicebox. Roger was in the midst of a very intent circle and would not leave to take a swim in the river with Adam. Feeling rather uneasy, the boy called to Nick and went off by himself.

On the way back, with his hair dripping in his eyes and Nick shaking a shower all over him, he met his father coming toward him. Even from a distance Adam could tell that Roger was feeling very gloomy. He walked heavily and his shoulders drooped, his chin was on his chest, his mouth was down at the corners, and his brows were drawn almost together over his eyes.

"Have you got your purse still?" he called to Adam.

"Yes, it's here in my wallet. Do you want it?"

"No, boy, I don't. Keep it close and don't let it out of your hands. Even if I ask you for it don't give it to me. I'm not to be trusted with money. I lost mine at dice to Jankin."

"Oh!" exclaimed Adam, his face falling. All those silver pennies and nothing at all in exchange for them!

"What's worse, trying to get the silver back, I lost Bayard."

Bayard, *Bayard!* Adam fought the tears back. Oh well, he told himself, we never had a horse before. Oh well, we've still got Nick.

"Say it," said Roger irritably. "Say something!"

When at length it came, what Adam said made no sense at all to Roger.

"It will be pretty hard," said Adam, "on Hugh."

Red in the Morning

O̲N THE second morning after the wedding Adam and Roger and Nick set forth on foot. It was still so early that each blade of grass had its drop of dew glistening in the sun and each little tuft and hummock its shadow. Adam's heart lifted to meet the new day. Where would he sleep that night? He did not know. He only knew that the road lay before him, and in its turns and hollows new sights and adventures were waiting.

"It will rain before night," said Roger. "The sun rose red."

"I've got my cloak," said Adam. "I can keep my harp dry under that."

He had his other cotte and breeches tied up in his cloak and hung on his back. His coverlet he had had to leave behind with Matthew, who promised to keep it for him. The big portmanteau had been left too, and Roger carried a smaller bag like a pilgrim's scrip.

Beyond the gates of de Lisle House, they turned to the right toward London. Roger, who was in one of his silent moods this morning, lengthened his stride, and Adam had to quicken his steps to keep up. Nick, with his nose to the ground, ran a zigzag course ahead of them. Not many people were on the road; Adam saw only an apprentice hurrying on an errand, a carter with a load of wood, a couple of gray-robed, barefoot friars.

"I wish the Bishop of Lichfield would come out of his house," he said. "We've lived near him for almost two months, and I've never once seen him."

"Why on earth do you want to see the Bishop of Lichfield?" said Roger.

"Why, I told you!" Grown-ups were queer, even Roger. If they told you anything, they expected you to remember it forever after, but when you told them something, half the time they forgot it so thoroughly that they did not even remember that they had ever heard it. "I want to see him so I can tell Perkin. His name is Walter Langton and Perkin says he started out a poor man. He studied the law and now he's the king's adviser. Perkin is going to be just like him."

Roger only said "Humph," to this; Roger was feeling very low in his mind, Adam knew, about the loss of Bayard. Hugh had been dreadfully disturbed too, when he heard. "Now I'll never get Bayard back," he said bitterly. (Exactly what he meant by that, Adam thought it best not to inquire.) "That Jankin fellow," Hugh had continued, "doesn't know one thing about horses. He'll ride Bayard to death. Why in the world couldn't Roger hold on to him after he got him?"

Later Hugh had said rather grumpily, "It isn't your fault, Adam, you've been decent about it," but things were not the same as they had been. It was almost like that first day when they had come from St. Alban's.

Adam missed Bayard himself, but on the whole he preferred walking to riding. The portmanteau behind the saddle was not very comfortable, and he felt uneasy about Nick all the time he was riding.

"I bet I can walk all day now without getting tired," he said as they went under the wooden bar that the Knights Templars had set up across the road. "I couldn't have when I was at St. Alban's. Studying makes you soft, but all the tilting and swimming and racing and wrestling I've been doing has hardened me up again. Look at my muscle." He tightened his fist and crooked his arm. "Look, Roger, feel it!"

Roger looked down at his son and after a moment he smiled. He felt the hard and bulging muscle. "Wonderful!" he said. "I hope your mind hasn't gone soft while your body's been hardening. Sir Edmund gave me some writing in Latin that I want you to read. My Latin's rusty."

"Now?"

"Later, when we can find a place to sit down and spread it out."

The bridge over Fleet Stream was the real boundary of London, though Ludgate lay a bit ahead on the hill. Adam called Nick to heel, for already there were more people about and carts and horsemen, and they crossed over the narrow river that emptied into the Thames between the house of the White Friars and the house of the Black Friars.

Adam exclaimed, as he always did at the first whiff of the air in the city, "I know now why Sir Edmund would rather live in the Strand. London smells!"

It smelled of the pigs and cows and chickens that roamed at large. It smelled of the garbage that lay rotting in the middle of the streets. It smelled of the people who lived so close together. In some places the streets were so narrow and the upper stories of the houses hung so far out over them that the sun never got through to sweeten things up. Adam's nose, used to clean fresh air and country odors, wrinkled in disgust. Soon, however, he became used to the smell and even forgot about it.

The mighty cathedral of St. Paul's loomed up before them with the sun shining on the copper-gilt eagle that crowned its spire. Here was no quiet church removed from the stress of active life; this was a powerful temple of God in the heart of a busy city, swarming with people and noisy with their concerns.

"Let's go in," said Roger. "I'll show you that parchment."

Adam fastened Nick's leash to his collar and they went in at the west door. Even inside, it was not quiet. The middle aisle, which was called "Paul's Walk," was full of people all apparently transacting important business. Adam saw three men of law in sober mantles walking up and down, talking and gesticulating. He saw a red-faced merchant stride up to another who had just entered and shout angrily, "Where have you been? I've been waiting all morning for you." He saw two bearded knights in full armor come clanking through the crowd, while a baker's boy with a basket of bread on his arm darted out of their way.

"Sooner or later," said Roger, "you see everybody you know in Paul's Walk."

High above the din of voices and scuffling of feet the bells shook out a cascade of rich golden sounds that ran in and out of each other joyously. People knew how to cast wonderful bells in the thirteenth century. From a chapel far down the long cathedral came beautiful, ordered singing.

Roger led Adam to a window and took from his wallet a roll of parchment, which he spread out on top of a carved stone knight who lay with his feet crossed. It was the tomb of a man who had died in the first Crusade, but his shield made a very good table.

"See," said Roger. "Sir Edmund gave me this to show to any of his friends whom we may meet along the way. What does it say?"

Adam studied the square black letters that marched neatly across the parchment. "Salutem et amoris perpetui firmitatem," he read, and translated slowly, 'Greetings and assurances of perpetual love.' "

"Skip all that part. What does he say about me?"

" 'Egregium instrionem — egregium means towering above the flock — outstanding minstrel — qui nuper meae filiae interfuit nuptiis — who was at the recent marriage of my daughter — ubi suum officium exercuit eleganter — where he exercised his office elegantly — ad vos cum magna confidentia destinamus — we recommend to you with great confidence.' That's fine, isn't it?"

"Is there anything more?"

"Yes. I can't read every word, but he asks them to give you aliquid subsidium — some subsidy — and then there's something about special grace."

Roger rolled the parchment up and put it carefully into the leather wallet hanging on his belt. "That will do nicely," he said. "Especially," he added with a flicker of a smile, "the subsidy. Well, come on, egregium instrionem, we'd best be on our way."

"I wish he had put something about Nick

in it," said Adam, starting to walk off without noticing that Nick had sat down for a good scratch. The jerk of the leash all but upset him. "He could have said egregium instrionem et eius egregium canem."

Roger flicked Adam's turned-up nose with his finger. "How about his outstanding son?" he said.

When they came out of the south door of St. Paul's into the garth, they found that the sun had disappeared behind some spreading clouds and the air was chilly. They walked down Dere Street, which the Romans had built, to Cannon Street, where the London Stone stood, which was so old that nobody knew who had put it there. All along the way Adam was saying, "Look, Roger! That huckster has some brambleberries!" and "Roger, they're going to have bean pottage in that house, I smell it cooking!" and finally, "Roger, I'm hungry!"

Then Roger took him to the cook shop on the Thames near Botolph's Wharf. It was the most amazing place Adam had ever seen; it existed only to sell hot food to people who lived elsewhere. There was a room with two long tables and benches, and at the end of it a wide opening into another room where furiously busy cooks ran to and fro against a background of blazing fires. Roger led Adam to a place near a window and called for roasted capon.

A rather greasy-looking overgrown boy set a cup of ale and a small loaf of bread before each of them and went back to the kitchen. Adam took his knife out of his wallet and prepared his bread carefully; first he cut the whole loaf in half, then he cut the top part in four, and put the pieces together as if they were whole, and turned the bottom half down to make a trencher for his meat. After that he sat up very straight and looked about him. Hungry as he was, he would not be so impolite as to touch bread or ale before his meat came, lest he should seem either starved or a glutton.

Across the table a round-faced chapman was eating fatted goose with parsley, and down the room a bit, a monk in a brown robe attacked a large and steaming beef pie. The delicious odors of roasting meat filled Nick with longing. He stood up and put his paws on Adam's knee, giving a sigh so deep that it was almost a groan. When his portion of capon was set before him, Adam cut off a piece for Nick, and slipped it down under the table to him. After that it was a race between

them, with Adam losing, for Nick ate his bits
with a snap and a swallow and was back asking for more before Adam could chew his
mouthful up.

The food was good. Not for many minutes
did Adam speak. "The only thing I don't like
about this," he said at length, batting the air
before his face with his hand, "is the flies."

Nick, as if to say that he agreed, jumped
up and snapped at one. His leash slipped off
Adam's knees. The fly buzzed away, and
Nick followed, leaping and snapping.

"Here, Nick," called Adam. "Come back."

Nick, at the door, met a familiar pair of
legs, which he paused to sniff at.

"There's Jankin," whispered Adam. "Here,
Nick!"

Roger turned to look. The minstrel caught
his eye and came over to the table. Nick
trotted along with him, and when Jankin
flung his leg over the bench and sat down,
the little dog stood up beside him to get his
ears scratched.

"That's a good dog," said Jankin. He took
a silver penny from his purse and tossed it
up into the air, caught it on one hand, and
clapped it on the back of the other without
uncovering it. "I'll match you for him," he

said. "Call cross twice out of three and you get the war horse back. Fail, and I get the dog."

"No," said Roger shortly. "The dog belongs to the boy."

Adam glowered at Jankin, and snapped his fingers commandingly at Nick. Nick came to him and Adam picked up the leash. "Sit down," he said, and Nick sat, his silky body pressed close against Adam's legs.

Jankin called for beef and leeks and ale, and then rested his elbows on the table and leaned forward. "Which way are you going?" he said. Evidently the subject of Nick was closed.

"Across London Bridge," said Roger briefly.

"Winchester?"

"Maybe."

"Giles's Fair?"

Adam held his breath, waiting for Roger's answer. Giles's Fair was the greatest fair in England. It came once a year and lasted for three weeks, and people from all over Europe brought their best wares to sell there. If they were going to Giles's Fair, that *would* be something to look forward to!

Roger grunted so that Adam could not tell whether he meant yes or no.

Jankin yawned. "That's where I'm going," he said, "but don't worry, it's big enough for both of us. Any time you want another game of dice, I'm your man."

Roger stood up. "I play no more dice," he said. "Come, Adam."

Adam, holding Nick short on the leash, followed his father out of the cook shop and down to the wharf, where they stood and looked at the gray, ship-filled river. On their left the Tower of London loomed up with surrounding gray walls and a tall white-washed tower very high and clean against the dingy clouds.

"It looks like rain," said Adam.

Still Roger said nothing.

"Are we going to Giles's Fair?" ventured Adam.

"Yes, there's a good chance for minstrelsy there," answered Roger, putting his hand on Adam's shoulder.

"I don't like that Jankin," declared Adam. "He wanted to get Nick! Hugh said he'd probably ride Bayard to death. Would he, Roger, do you think?"

Roger's hand tightened on his shoulder. "Hush," he said. "Your voice carries too well. Look at the ships and think what they're bringing to London — wine from France and woad to make blue dye and all kinds of fine silks and spices, and shellfish — "

"When will we get to Winchester?" interrupted Adam.

"Never, unless we make a start."

As they turned away from the wharf toward London Bridge, it began to rain.

Night in Westhumble Lane

FOR the rest of that day and all the next it
rained. They walked southwest over the
low-lying meadows and fields and woodland
of the Thames valley, with the rain pattering
steadily in their faces. It was the time of the
grain harvest, but nobody could work in the
fields in this downpour. Where the grain had
already been cut, flocks of lapwings with
black belts hunted about for food among the
scarlet poppies in the stubble. In the villages
men went from stable to barn with sacking
over their heads, or stood in the shelter of
doorways to talk.

Adam's green hood with its short cape kept

his head and shoulders fairly dry and the harp that bulged in the middle of his back, but by the second afternoon his legs were wet to the knees and his shoes squelched at every step. Nick was soaked too. The light hair on his stomach was dark mud-colored; all the feathers on his legs were like dripping rattails; he plodded along with his head low, and now and then he stopped and shook himself violently, sending a muddy shower all over Adam.

"Nick never thinks of going off by himself to shake," grumbled Adam, wiping his cheek with the back of his hand.

"Watch out!" cried Roger.

They both jumped to the road's edge just as a man on horseback clattered round the curve behind them and without slackening his pace pounded down the road ahead. His horse's hoofs splashed up mud in blobs. Nick took off after the horse, and Adam, almost breathless with shocked surprise, called him back.

"Best put him on the leash," said Roger. "He's been trained to follow Bayard, and he might go on doing it from force of habit."

"Was that Bayard?"

"Bayard it was, and Master Jankin showing off for all he was worth. Wellaway! I

wish we had Bayard now. His iron shoes would save our leather ones on these muddy roads. Can you hold out a few miles farther? There's an inn at Burford Bridge where we can lie tonight."

"Ho!" said Adam stoutly, "I could walk ten miles more."

It would be fun to spend the night at an inn. Last night they had slept at Merton Priory on the River Wandle. They had been comfortable there, and Adam had thought it good to hear again the bells ringing for compline and matins and prime and the monks' voices chanting the services, but there had been no one in the little guesthouse but themselves and two sleepy peddlers who cared nothing for minstrelsy.

Nick indicated by bracing his four feet suddenly that he did not think it was fair to be leashed on a country road. Adam pulled him along sitting down until the sight of the collar around Nick's ears and the alarmed but determined look in Nick's eyes melted his never stony heart. "There," he said, and undid the thing. Nick rewarded him with a brisk shower of mud and trotted off to the roadside with one ear turned up over his head.

"What kind of folk will there be at the inn tonight?" said Adam.

"Pilgrims, perhaps, going to Canterbury, or merchants going to the fair at Winchester."

"What tale shall we tell them?"

"Well," answered Roger slowly, "which one do you think they'd like best?"

Adam thought a bit as he splashed along in the rain, jumping a puddle here and straddling one there. "Not a French one, I shouldn't think," he answered at last. "'Cause why, there wouldn't be knights and ladies at an inn and they're the ones that like stories about love and chivalry. I'm tired of 'Sir Orfeo' and 'Floris and Blanchefleur' and 'Aucassin and Nicolette' anyhow. I don't want to hear about any more ladies leaving little bunches of flowers in the forest for their lovers to find them by. Let's tell 'King Horn' and have some good shipwrecks."

Roger laughed. "There speaks an Englishman," he said. "We shall tell 'King Horn,' and in English. No French at Burford Bridge."

The road had been going steadily uphill for some time, for they were on the long gradual slope that led to the chalk ridge called the North Downs. Yew trees grew black and gloomy against the rain-filled sky; the soft wet wind blew without ceasing. A magpie, very big and black and white, flashed across the road in front of them.

"One for sorrow," said Roger, half to himself.

"Two for mirth," answered Adam quickly. "We'll see another one in a minute. You watch that side of the road and I'll watch this."

He could not bear to think of sorrow when they were so happy. Even wet, even footsore, they were happy. His quick eyes saw a rabbit sitting up on its hind legs among the ferns, they saw a man with a cow far down the road ahead, they saw a lark rise out of the field. They forgot to look for the second magpie.

Presently the road went steeply down hill. At the bottom lay the river Mole, and the stone bridge, and a cluster of houses, and a church. Roger went straight to the little inn in Westhumble Lane, which had a moon and stars painted on the signboard that swung and creaked in the rain.

The innkeeper's wife, whose name was Clarice, took Adam in charge at once. She was a spidery, active little woman with bright black eyes. She had two maids and a man and a boy working for her, not to mention her husband. She flung out orders like blows, and they all, Adam noticed, dodged them as if they had been blows.

"Fetch me a bucket from the well," she commanded. "Bring me a towel. And turn the cake on the hearth. I smell it burning. Poor boy! Mud from head to foot. See that the man in the front room doesn't get away without paying. A scrubbing, that's what you need, and dry clothing. Can you play that harp — a little fellow like you? Stir the pottage, Maud, we've minstrels in the house tonight."

For a moment Adam, smarting over being called a little fellow, was afraid that she was going to strip him and scrub him then and there in the crowded kitchen, but she didn't. Roger got the bucket from the well, and Dame Clarice herself went for the towel. Then she showed them a shed in the stable-yard where they could wash in privacy, while she bustled off to turn the cake herself, and collect money from the man in the front room and stir the pottage as it ought to be stirred.

Adam and Roger bathed and put on the

extra clothes which were in Roger's bag. Adam, who was dressed first, took their wet garments into the kitchen, which, with the firelight and the fragrance of good food cooking, was a cheerful place on this rainy afternoon. A baby lay in a wooden cradle; its very young, red-cheeked mother sat beside it with a distaff and spindle, and with steadily twisting fingers made the bunch of wool on the distaff into the thread wound on the spindle. A young man brought in a pail of milk and stopped to tickle the baby's chin with his big horny forefinger. A maid came in to get bread and cheese from a cupboard and went out again. Dame Clarice bustled about with a long iron spoon in her hand, which seemed to be equally useful for stirring the pot and nudging people out of her way.

Adam spread out their wet clothes on a bench in front of the fire, then sat down beside them to see that they did not scorch. His shoes he put on the hearth and tucked his feet in their cloth hose under him. Nick lay down on his back on the hearth and waved his feet comfortably in the warm glow.

"How old are you, boy?" A voice from the corner made Adam jump.

He had not seen the old man who sat there.

He was a very old man; his hair was white and the wrinkles around his frosty blue eyes looked as if they had been made in parchment, but there was a kind of shine in his smile.

"I'm eleven, sir," said Adam.

"I was just about as big as you are when King John signed the Charter at Runnymede seventy-nine years ago. I lived down the road a bit near Reigate Castle. My father was heyward on the lard's demesne. Do you know what a heyward is, Londoner?"

"Yes, sir. He sees the hedges are mended and keeps the cows and sheep out of the grain, and people too."

Dame Clarice took up Adam's cloak, shook it briskly, and put it back again. "Gaffer is always at it," she said. "Telling about his boyhood to anyone that has time to listen."

"Let me tell the lad," persisted the old man irritably. "He'll like it. His mind isn't on cooking."

"Please tell me, sir," said Adam politely, remembering the proverb of Alfred that his father had taught him:

"If you sit upon the bench
    And see before you standing

A trembling old man,
Get up from your seat
And bid him sit down.
Then will he say
'A good man taught you first.'
Then sit afterward
Beside him, and learn wisdom."

"I was a wild boy," said the old gaffer. "I knew every bush and stump and stone, and I knew the cave under the castle courtyard. I knew the barons were meeting in secret all through May that year. Earl William was thought to be the king's man, but he was meeting there with these others in the cave beneath the courtyard."

Adam really listened, now that it was a matter of caves.

"Then one day," the old man went on, "a man came stamping through the north barley field, and my father blew his horn and stopped him. He would have taken his hood or his gloves from him in penalty for tramping through the lord's grain, but that he showed the badge of a king's messenger. He could take any short cut he wanted. Eh, but my father was angry — all that barley stamped down and no more than a quarter of a mile saved by his shortcut. But he could do nothing."

"What happened next?" asked Adam, caring nothing for the barley.

"I ran quick to the entrance to the cave and told the squire on guard that the messenger was coming. He didn't stop to ask how I got there. He ran! When the messenger reached the castle, there was Earl William in the solar reading to his lady."

"What was in the message?"

"That I don't know, but it wasn't long after that the barons left. Not all at once, and not openly. Earl William rode out last of all. Then we heard that they met the king at Runnymede and forced him to sign the Charter. He said afterward that he signed it under duress and so it didn't bind him, but King John is dead these many years — may God have mercy on his soul — and the freedom the Great Charter won for us lives in England still. It was a day early in June that the messenger came. I'm nearly ninety now, but I've never forgotten it. Keep your eyes open, boy. You may see big things happening."

"Yes, sir," said Adam, his eyes shining.

He had no idea what the Great Charter might be, but the thought of barons meeting in a cave and a boy of his own age running to warn them set every nerve in his body to tingling.

"The boy's a minstrel," scolded Dame Clarice, coming back with her spoon to stir again. "You should let him tell you tales."

"All the adventures don't happen in minstrels' tales. Let the boy keep his eyes open, he may see great things happen, though he won't know it at the time. Now, I've done."

He had done too. He folded his wrinkled hands over his stomach, closed his eyes, and went to sleep.

Adam put his shoes on silently and stole away from the fire, which had become too hot.

He found Roger in the front room perched on the edge of a bed talking to a chapman who was sitting on his trunk, wringing out his wet hood, and grumbling about the weather.

Gradually the inn filled up. Besides the chapman there were two merchants with packhorses and servants, and two fellows of a college at Oxford with their servants and horses, and a carpenter who had been on a pilgrimage to Canterbury and had a little lead picture of St. Thomas sewn in his cap. Dame Clarice was busier than ever, and even her lazy helpers bestirred themselves. Everybody wanted supper at the same time.

The chapman and the carpenter had bread and cheese and ale. The merchants had hot spiced wine and meat with a savory sauce. The clerks from Oxford had bread and beef and gravy and ale. Adam and Roger had bread and pottage, and very good it was too. The bread was made of flour from the new wheat just harvested. Bread always tasted best in August, Adam thought, partly because it really was so good and sweet and fresh, and partly because the bread in July, made from what was left of last year's flour, was often musty and sour.

When they had eaten Roger nodded to Adam, and he drew his fingers over his harp strings. One of the clerks leaned back against the wall and crossed his legs. "Minstrels," he said to his companion. "Good. I'm not ready to sleep and we can't read unless we pay for candles."

The room was dim with the rain and the gathering dark. Dame Clarice's man came in with a torch which he set in a holder on the stone wall. It gave a wavering and murky light that fell on Roger's face, making deep caverns of his eyes and little shadowed hollows under his cheekbones.

"Listen, lordings," he began, and paused while Dame Clarice and her daughter, and the maids and the men came into the room. Then he went on, "Hearken, wives and maidens, and all men, to my story of Murry, king of the western land, and his son Horn. Sun never shone and rain never rained on a fairer lad. He was bright as glass and ruddy and brave, and when my tale begins he was fifteen winters old. He had twelve companions, all rich men's sons, and all fair lads."

Adam thought of Hugh and Godfrey and the rest, and of Perkin. Wouldn't they open their eyes if they could see him now!

"It was on a summer day that Murry, the good king, rode by the seaside with two of his knights. There he saw fifteen ships come sailing right to the shore.

"The ships were full of Saracens. They slew Murry and put the queen to flight. They took Horn and his companions prisoners. Their leader spoke. 'Horn, you are tall and shining; in seven years you will grow still bigger. If we let you and your companions live, you may kill us all. Therefore you must put to sea in a ship, and if the ship sinks to bottom and drowns you, every one, we shall not regret it.' "

The ship — and the story — were launched. Adam listened as if he did not know every turn of it. Roger never told it quite the same way. Sometimes he dwelt on Horn's love for the princess Rymenhild, sometimes on his friendship with Athulf; this time it was the sea he dwelt on, and the storms and the ships that sailed over it.

When he reached the fight between Horn and the pagan knight, he stopped in the middle of a sentence. "Good friends," he said, "give me some reward for my art, and I will continue."

Adam snatched off his cap and went with it from one person to another. One merchant put in half of a silver penny; the other hesitated, but when Adam made Nick stand up and ask for it, he laughed and threw in a penny. The clerks from Oxford gave a penny between them, the chapman shook his head, the carpenter left the room, the inn servants grinned, and Dame Clarice said, "A bed's my gift, even though I can't throw it in the cap."

Roger went on with the tale.

Before it was finished, Jankin came in. He looked pale in the torchlight, and his mouth had a bitter droop to it. He called for ale and supped it noisily, and when Roger had come to the end of the tale, he called out, "Your tale limps like your horse, minstrel."

"My horse never limped when I rode him," snapped Roger. "Have you lamed him galloping like mad over steep roads?"

"He's lame," said Jankin shortly. "I thought to be in Guildford tonight but I had to come back, the horse limping and I walking. More ale, dame!"

Bayard lame! Won from them, and ridden carelessly, and lamed! Roger and Adam went to bed in heavy silence.

Several beds in the room were already filled, but the one nearest the door was left for them. Adam took off his surcoat and his shoes, and scrambled over the straw to the far side. Straw and coverlet were both thin, but they were clean and dry too, and Roger was there beside him. He hung his hand over the edge of the bed, and Nick, who had curled up on the floor, licked it softly. Poor Bayard, thought Adam, cupping his palm around Nick's muzzle. Then he pressed his finger lightly on Nick's moist cool nose and scratched a little the silky hollow between his eyes. Nick licked his hand again, and he pulled it back into bed because that last kiss had been a little too wet.

He could not know that he was saying good-bye to Nick.

"Here, Nick!"

ADAM fell into sleep so deep that it was like going down into a well like a bucket. He heard none of the sounds made by the other people in the room. Some of them snored; some tossed and turned in their beds; one of them got up early. He did not hear that one snap his fingers at Nick, nor hear Nick come out obligingly from under the bed, stretching first his legs and then his neck and finishing with a yawn that shook him to the toes. He did not even stir when a strong hand clasped Nick around the muzzle to silence him and a strong arm scooped him up in one swift motion. After that there was nothing to hear but the tiptoeing footsteps of the man — and there are always footsteps in an inn.

When at length Adam stirred and opened his eyes, the sun was coming through the little windows and in every bed one or two people were sitting up and yawning and stretching. Adam sat up too and rubbed his eyes with his knuckles and stretched his arms as far as they would go, until suddenly he was wide awake.

He saw Roger sitting on the side of the bed looking troubled.

"Son," said Roger, and that alarmed Adam because Roger called him "Son" only when his feelings were deeply stirred, "I am afraid the dog is gone."

"Nick?" Fear struck at Adam's heart, but his mind refused to accept it. "He wouldn't run away." He hung over the side of the bed till his topknot grazed the floor and the blood thumped in his ears, and looked under the bed, under the whole row of beds. Shoes were there, worn and scuffed and curling at the toes and lying on their sides, but no Nick. Adam pulled himself up again.

"Nick! Here, Nick!" he called.

His face had turned white and every freckle stood out; his gray eyes were nearly black. "Nick!"

The other people in the room began to take an interest. They looked on the floor under their beds or shook their heads and said, "Tck, tck," or suggested that Nick had gone outdoors. One of them said to Roger in a low voice, "That fellow's gone — the other minstrel."

Adam scrambled into his hose and shoes and hustled on his surcoat, leaving his harp and belt and wallet for his father to gather up. He rushed out of doors.

"Nick!" he called. "Nick!"

After the rain all the leafy world was washed and sparkling. There were chickens in the road and ducks waddling in a solemn row to the river.

"Here, Nick!" cried Adam. Even as he called he knew that it was useless. Nick would not have gone away unless he had been taken.

He heard a cart grinding and grating along the road and soon saw its nail-studded wheels kicking up great dollops of mud. He ran to meet it.

"Good morrow, sir!" he cried. "Have you seen a red spaniel?"

The carter was an old man with white hair and white whiskers round his chin. He stopped and looked at Adam with quizzical blue eyes.

"Now, young sir," he said slowly, "I *have* seen a red spaniel, many a red spaniel in my time, but not today, nor yet yesterday. Have you lost one?"

Adam did not wait for the rest of this useless speech, but ran back to the inn, where various well-meaning people were darting about whistling shrilly. As if, thought Adam scornfully, Nick would come for them instead of me!

In the kitchen he found Roger and the inn-wife and the maids all gathered round a stableboy who hung his head and shuffled his feet and muttered sullenly in answer to half a dozen questions, all noisily shouted at once.

"Here," said Roger. "This is serving no purpose. Leave the boy to me, and he will tell me what I need to know."

With one arm over Adam's shoulder and with the other hand kindly but firmly on the back of the stableboy's neck, he led them both out into the stable yard. Adam, looking up at his father's face, saw there a grim determination that somewhat comforted him.

When they were out of earshot of the crowd gaping in the kitchen door, they stopped. "Now," said Roger, "there's nothing to be afraid of. Just tell me what happened."

"He c-came out before sunup," said the boy, stuttering a little. "The other minstrel, that was. He had the dog under his arm and he said he'd made a trade with you, the dog for the war horse. And then he went."

"Which way did he go?"

"Over the bridge and up the track toward Ranmore Common. The horse is in the stable. I didn't do nothing, sir."

The innkeeper and the others edged out of the kitchen and across the yard in time to hear the end of this. They all had their comments to make, the gist of which was that a war horse, even a lame one, was a good exchange for a red spaniel any day.

"You made a shrewd bargain there, minstrel," said the merchant. He was a smooth, prosperous-looking man with round little red cheeks above a curly beard; he wore rich clothes and his hands were soft and plump like little pink pigs. Adam looked at him in rage.

"There's no war horse in the world that's half as good as Nick!" he cried, and stopped. Bayard was a good horse; they had missed him sorely. Could Roger — ? He clutched his father's arm. "You didn't — ?" he began breathlessly.

"No, Adam, no."

Adam looked deep into Roger's true gray eyes, and knew that never in the world would he have secretly traded Nick for any horse. For a moment Adam felt overcome with shame at having harbored such a thought, then he forgot it as the realization of Nick stolen flooded his soul with anguish.

"Come on!" he cried. "Come on! We've got to hurry. Maybe we can catch up with him."

"Who's going to pay for the horse?" said the innkeeper. "A penny a day for fodder it will cost. And he ought to have a poultice on his leg."

Every minute Jankin was taking Nick farther along the road. Adam looked down at his shadow, which stretched thin and black over the straw-strewn muck of the farmyard and bent up the side of the stable. It was a long shadow still, but every minute was shortening it, and Jankin had started before there were any shadows at all.

Bayard whinnied, and Roger, with Adam protesting at his heels, went to look at him. The horse was lame, there was no doubt of that, too lame to move. Adam tugged at Roger's sleeve. "Oh, come on," he implored. "We can come back for Bayard. Let's go get Nick now."

They had the reckoning to pay and an endless deal of advice, it seemed, to receive. They were off at last, with packets of bread and cheese and cold meat in their wallets. Across the stone bridge they went, and up the steep slope of Ranmore Common, along the old track under the brow of the hill that the people of England had been using for centuries and centuries. Long before the Romans came, the Britons had brought their ingots of tin from Cornwall in the west over this high road to the eastern harbors. They called it a highway because it ran high along the chalk ridge that stretched across southern England. Now it was the Pilgrims' Way from Winchester to Canterbury.

This morning it was full of sky and sun and wind. As Adam and Roger crushed the little gray leaves of the thyme under their feet, the sun shone on the bruised leaves and brought out their fragrance, and the warm wind spread it far and wide. Below them stretched the Weald, that low-lying, clayey land grown over with thick forests of oak, and away at the southern horizon's edge was the blue line of hills called the South Downs, and beyond them a misty silver streak that Roger said was the sea. Now and then as they hurried along the ancient track they passed into the shade of yew trees.

Adam strained his eyes ahead along the road, looking always for a wiry figure and a little dog. He strained his body too, hurrying always, and breathing hard. Nick, his thoughts went, over and over, Nick! We've got to hurry. We've got to catch up with him!

They met a shepherd.

"Have you seen a minstrel with a red spaniel?" cried Adam.

No, the shepherd had seen neither minstrel nor dog.

They met a pardoner, with pilgrim's badges sewn all over his cap and coat, and bag of pardons hanging on his back.

"Have you seen a minstrel with a red spaniel?" asked Adam.

In the same moment the pardoner began

to talk about the wares which he had to sell, pardons from Rome. Pay a few pence and buy a pardon for your sins.

"Jankin should have one of those," said Adam grimly.

"Who is he? Where is he?" asked the pardoner.

"That's what I'd like to know," said Adam. "He's got my dog. Have you seen a little red spaniel?"

But the pardoner cared nothing for little red spaniels. He went on his way.

"Sit down and rest now," said Roger after a while. "You'll save time in the end."

They had crossed Ranmore Common and come out on the White Downs. Ahead of them the track stretched in broken white lines where the underlying chalk showed through the turf. Adam flung himself down on the ground and buried his hot face in the fresh grass. All within him was turmoil; his thoughts and feelings buzzed like angry bees, and like bees they stung him hotly.

Roger sat beside him. "Never fear," he said consolingly. "We'll get him back."

Adam rolled over and sat up, unconscious of his face streaked with dust and tears. "Where has he gone, do you think? Why hasn't anybody seen him? Look, there's a church tower down there in the trees. There must be a village! Maybe he's there."

"He'd only have to come back to the Pilgrims' Way. There's no road through the Weald. Most likely he's going to Guildford over yonder."

He gestured with his hands, but Adam saw nothing but the round-topped downs tumbling over one another against the sky. While he gazed, a knot of figures far in the distance slowly detached itself from the background and began to grow steadily larger. Adam soon saw that there were twelve or more men and women on horseback.

"Pilgrims," said Roger. "We'll ask them. Pilgrims always see everything."

He stood up as they drew near, and so did Adam. The first two were jolly and substantial-looking townsfolk, and behind them were two countrymen.

"God save this merry company," said Roger politely.

"Sir, God save you," replied the nearest pilgrim.

Adam stepped forward. "Have you seen a minstrel with a red spaniel?" he asked, and his eagerness caught in his throat and almost choked him.

"We have a pack of minstrels following on our heels. Look for yourself, boy."

Adam ran to the end of the calvacade, where he did indeed see three or four minstrels of the poorer sort, and three dogs. One was a greyhound, and one was a very fat, very old brown and white spaniel, and one was a little thin scrawny creature with a tail bigger than he was.

One of the minstrels winked at Adam and jerked his head backward. "On your way, boy," he said. "We need no more harpers here. These worthy pilgrims have no soul for music — "

"Have you seen a minstrel with a red spaniel?" interrupted Adam.

"And what pennies they part with for tales shall go to us," finished the minstrel calmly. "You mean Jankin of Chester?"

"With a dog at the end of a leash?" put in another.

"And wings on his feet," added a third, "and never a civil word in his mouth?"

"Yes!" cried Adam. "That's the one. Where did you met him?"

"Near Saint Martha's Chapel an hour or

more ago. We chaffed him about his dog."

"That's *my* dog!" cried Adam in such a heartbroken voice that at once all the minstrels lost their jesting air and the hindermost of the pilgrims reined in his horse and came back.

They were all so full of sympathy and so eager to know just what had happened that Adam had difficulty in getting them to answer his questions.

"He was two years old," he answered impatiently. "Please, where was he going? Yes, Jankin took him while I was sleeping at the inn last night. Please, which road was he taking? It was the inn at Burford Bridge. Please, did he say where he was going?"

Then Roger came up and settled it. "We're for Guildford in a hurry," he said briskly. "Farewell, friends, have good day."

He clapped Adam on the shoulder and they strode off.

"I got it from the wife of the first pilgrim," said Roger. "They met Jankin where the road divides and he asked the shortest way to Guildford. She noticed the dog. He was so soft and shiny, she said, and friendly."

"That was Nick all right," said Adam, half proudly, half sadly.

"Jankin will sleep tonight at Guildford," Roger went on. "We're sure to find him there."

It sounded very definite. Even the names of the places along the way gave Adam confidence. They would find Nick again. Of course they would. He stepped out stoutly.

Adam Swims the Wey

THE road led down into the valley of a winding river fringed with trees. Roger would have been glad to stop and bathe here, but Adam urged him on.

"When we get to Guildford we still have to hunt for Jankin!" he cried. "He might get out of town before we find him."

"This is a good place to eat our dinner," said Roger.

They lay down at the edge of the stream and plunged their heads into the cool water. Coming up dripping and refreshed, they opened their wallets and took out the bread and cheese and cold meat. In spite of his impatience, Adam found that it tasted good.

When they had finished, Adam was eager to start right off again, but Roger stood looking down at him as if there was something he wanted to say. He wanted to tell his boy something about life and chance and the perils that beset beloved little dogs, but unable to find the words, he just stood there looking compassionate and helpless until Adam begged, "Let's hurry, Roger."

Under St. Martha's Hill the path divided. One branch went through the wood called Chantries and crossed the river Wey by a ferry south of Guildford, and the other led across Merrow Downs and over sunny Pewley Hill to the town. This was the shortest way to Guildford.

Adam's legs were tired as he stumped up the last rise in the chalky path, from which, in spite of yesterday's rain, a fine white dust was rising. They had come nearly twelve miles up hill and down, and the fever of fear that drove him on had given him energy, but it had wearied him too. Suppose they got to Guildford and couldn't find Nick after all! Suppose Jankin did not stop in Guildford but took a road right out of it to the south, or the north or the west. How would they know which road to follow?

Guildford was a busy little town of stone

and brick and timber clinging to the steep sides of the hill above the river Wey. It had three churches, and a castle where the sheriff of Surrey lived, and many inns, shops, and houses. Its streets were thronged with pilgrims and merchants, both English and foreign, on their way from Southampton to London, or from Winchester to Canterbury, and back again. The White Friars had a house there, and the Gray Friars too; the white or gray gowns mingled on the narrow streets with the bright-colored clothes of merchants and knights, and the green of the archers from the Castle.

Plenty of dogs were there in Guildford too: hunting dogs in pairs led by a huntsman, lap dogs lolling over the arms of their mistresses, stray mongrels snapping at people's heels and dodging kicks with their tails tucked in, now and then a spaniel trotting along busy and interested. Adam gathered fresh strength when he came into Guildford and saw all the people and the dogs. His eyes darted to right and left, and whenever he saw a spaniel his heart rose in his chest and flapped back again.

"How will we find him?" he said to Roger. "We can't stop everybody and ask."

"We'll try the inns and the marketplace, and then we'll go to the castle," said Roger. "It might be the Lord Sheriff would like some minstrelsy."

"Let's go to the castle first," suggested Adam. "I'll bet Jankin would go there first, when he's got Nick to show off."

Though he was pinning his hopes on the castle, he did not fail to look around every corner along the way and over every fence. He lagged quite a bit behind Roger, and was just going to run to catch up when he glanced down a rather unpromising little lane and saw something that brought him up short, tense in every fiber. It was just a glimpse, but it was unmistakable.

There, at the head of the lane, was the wiry figure of the minstrel Jankin and, balky at the end of a leash, the sturdy, silky, floppy-eared dog Nick. The next instant they whisked out of sight behind some barrels and a wall.

"There he is!" shouted Adam. "Roger, I see him!"

Without waiting for an answer, off he shot down the lane, splashing through mud puddles and leaping over piles of trash.

Roger, who had not been paying attention,

turned his head, but not quickly enough to see where Adam had gone. As far as he was concerned, there were now two missing, a dog and a boy.

Adam ran down the lane, lickety-split, and turned the corner where the minstrel had disappeared so fast that he had to hold on to a barrel as he went past, to keep from swinging into the wall opposite.

A narrow passage went between the back of one house and a barn and pigsty that belonged to another. No one was in sight. Adam sped down this passage and came out on a little back street with brick and timber houses that seemed to be trying to touch foreheads across it. A small girl in a yellow frock came walking along with a loaf of bread in her arms, looking red in the face and cross.

"Little girl," Adam called, "have you seen a minstrel with a red spaniel?"

"Yes, I have. He jumped up and licked my loaf of bread. I don't like dogs."

"Where did he go?"

She pointed to a gate between two houses. "Through there."

Adam flung a thank-you over his shoulder, and burst through the wooden gate, letting it slam behind him. Stone steps with a mossy odor went steeply down between stone walls, and at the bottom he saw the river flowing.

Down he went, bounding from step to step like a stone rolling down a bumpy hill, grazing the palms of his hands on the rough walls as he used them for brakes.

When he reached the bottom he stopped and looked both ways. To the right he saw a narrow street leading to Guildford High Street and the bridge. To the left a little path followed the river past houses and under trees. In the distance, almost hidden by the low-hanging branches he saw a hurrying figure and a little dog trotting behind on a leash.

"Hi!" he shouted. "Hi, Jankin!"

He broke into a run.

In the curve of the path he lost Jankin for a minute, but when it straightened out again, there was Jankin far ahead running fast.

Soon Adam could run no more. He had come too far that day. When he slowed down, Jankin walked too.

So Adam pushed his way along the path by the river, seeing nothing, thinking of nothing but Jankin and the little dog ahead. Even after Jankin gained on him and got out of sight entirely, Adam plodded on. He was surprised when he came suddenly on a boat landing and found a group of people waiting there for the ferry.

"Have you seen a minstrel and a red spaniel?" he called.

A man pointed out over the river. The flat-bottomed ferryboat, poled by a man standing in the stern, was halfway across. In it were five or six people sitting very close together. One of them was a thin, dark, wiry man, and in his arms a red spaniel struggled to get free.

"There he is," said the man who pointed. "Came rushing up here, elbowing better folk aside, and jumped into the boat when it was full already and people waiting for the next trip. No manners. Friend of yours?"

"Nick!" shouted Adam. "Nick!"

There he was. There was Nick in that boat, and every minute the strip of water between them was widening. "That's my dog!" he cried. "He took my dog!"

The people on the dock at once gathered around him with exclamations and questions.

"When the ferry comes back, dearie," said a pleasant-faced woman, "you can have my place and I'll wait for the next one."

When the ferry came back! By that time Jankin would be gone, and Nick with him. They were nearly to the other shore now.

Adam took his harp from his shoulder and his bundle; he unfastened his belt and wallet and took off his shoes, and piled them all together. "Watch them for me," he said to the friendly woman.

Then he dived.

When he came up and blew the water out of his face he heard a babble of voices on the dock behind him, and saw the ferryboat with Nick and Jankin looming high in the water far in front of him. Then he set himself to the job of swimming to the other side. The current was swifter than he expected and his clothes were heavier. Furthermore, he had already had a long day, and he was tired. First his arms and legs felt like lead, then they felt like knives; then his breath got short. He swallowed a tankard or more of river water and coughed it out of his eyes and his nose and mouth. But he kept on kicking and splashing, and the next thing he knew, his knee hit something solid, and he found that he could stand up and wade the rest of the way.

Five or six staggering steps took him out

onto the bank where he fell on his face and panted and dripped.

Soon the thought of Nick jabbed him like an arrow. He sat up, wiped his wet face with his wet sleeve, shivered a little, and looked about him. The current had carried him downstream from the landing and the road. The ferryboat was already on its way back to the shore which he had left. He could see no one on this side, no one at all.

He wrung the water out of his surcoat as best he could, and squeezed all the gay fluttering points into wisps. He had no shoes, but his cloth hose were thick; they would serve till Roger followed with his things. The worst part, he found as he ran along the river's edge to the little landing place, was the way his wet hose picked up mud and gravel in cakes.

There was nobody at the landing place or the little house that stood in a garden beside it. Beyond the house was the forest. Adam looked at the narrow clay path that led straight into that thick wood of tall oaks and beech trees. Jankin must have gone that way. There was no other way for him to go.

The Ferryman's House

ADAM stood there between the wood and the river, shivering in his wet clothes. He could go no farther. His strength was spent.

The little house beside the boat-landing had a kindly look about it. Vines grew over its door, and sunflowers in the garden. Dragging his weary feet, Adam walked up the path and knocked at the door. After a moment he knocked again. No one answered.

A dog came around the side of the house, an old hound with long ears and drooping cheeks and sad eyes. He sniffed Adam thoroughly and then slowly and deliberately wagged his tail, batting it gently against Adam's legs. Adam scratched him in the places that he liked best, behind the ears and under the chin. With a sigh, the old dog lowered himself bone by bone to the ground where there was a patch of sunshine, and stretched out.

Adam sat down in the sun beside him, and tried to think. Somewhere ahead of him, pushing on through the forest, were Jankin and Nick. Somewhere behind him, beyond the river, was Roger. And here he was himself, alone, wet, without harp or shoes or wallet, and deathly tired. He would just wait here till Roger caught up with him.

The sun was warm, and the dog was friendly. Presently Adam put his head down on the dog and went to sleep.

Voices roused him. For a long time, it seemed, before he could really wake up, he heard them exclaiming over him.

"Eh, will you look at that. Sound asleep on old Colle."

"It's the boy that swam the river for his dog. Poor lad, he looks done in."

"Tck, tck, lying there in those wet clothes! Come, boy, wake up."

Somebody shook him by the shoulder, and the dog got out from underneath him. Wrenching his eyes open by main strength, he struggled to sit up. The woman on the landing place who had called him "dearie" was bending over him.

"Eh, that's better," she said. "Come into the house and sleep properly. See, I brought your things for you, your harp and shoes and wallet. Such a silly boy you were, thinking you could swim faster than the ferry!"

A man was with her, a big man with red hair and a brown wool tunic. "The boy looks worn out," he said. "What's your name, lad, and how far have you come today?"

"Adam, son of Roger the minstrel, sir." He tried to think back to that morning, but it seemed a hundred years ago. "We slept last night at Burford Bridge," he remembered at last.

"Burford Bridge!" The woman gave a horrified squawk, and the man stooped and swung Adam up in his arms.

He carried Adam into the house, where they peeled off his wet clothes, rolled him in a warm blanket, fed him hot bean pottage, and put him to bed in a little room upstairs where bunches of herbs were hung from the rafters to dry. The last thing Adam knew was the fragrance of those herbs and the sound of a kind voice saying, "Sleep well."

He almost woke when the first cock crew, and then again when the first party of pilgrims came to the river and called for the ferryman, but both times he rolled over and went back to sleep again. When at length, he opened his eyes and was all at once wide awake, he knew by the streaks of sunlight on the wooden wall and the daytime sounds below that the morning was well along. On a bench beside his bed he saw his clothes spread out, washed and dried, his shoes cleaned, his belt neatly folded and the wallet laid on top of it, his harp on the floor propped against the wall.

His first thought while he hurried into his clothes was that Roger had come and brought him his things. Doubtless he was even now downstairs waiting patiently for Adam to wake up. He hurried down some ladderlike steps that led to the room below, which, except for the sunshine and a few pieces of sturdy furniture, was empty. Out in the garden he found the good wife tending her beehives.

"Where's Roger?" he asked eagerly, without even stopping to say good morrow.

"Come away from the bees. They don't know you. Who is Roger?"

"Roger the minstrel, my father. Isn't he here? How did my things come here?"

"I brought them. No, lad, no minstrel has been here, except that one yesterday that had your dog. Are you sure your father knows were you are?"

For the first time it occurred to Adam that perhaps Roger did not know where he was. After all, he had just shouted and run, and it had been a very twisted way he followed, in and out among the barrels and back lanes, and along the winding river path. Perhaps Roger did not know where he was! Perhaps he was hunting all over Guildford!

"Oh," said Adam aghast, "I never thought of that! Oh, I must go right back to Guildford." Then he remembered that Jankin and Nick had gone through the wood in the opposite direction. "Where does this road go?" he asked, a little uncertainly.

She took a stick and drew a map on the ground. "Now here's Guildford and the bridge and the road to Farnham over the hill called the Hog's Back. And here's the ferry, up the river a bit from Guildford, and here's our house and our road. It runs through the woods to Whitewaysend, and there it joins the other road to Farnham."

Adam told her about Nick and Bayard and Jankin, and how he had lost Roger. She listened carefully, nodding her head from time to time.

"Now, likely that Jankin will go on to Farnham," she said. "It's a thriving town, with plenty of folk to hear minstrels' tales. Likely he will stay several days, when he think he's shaken you off. What you must do is go back to Guildford and find your father, and then you can go to Farnham together and find your dog."

It sounded wonderfully simple and easy as she said it. Adam took heart.

"Here comes John Ferryman now for his dinner," said his wife. "You must eat with us before you go back to Guildford."

It was a happy house. John Ferryman and his wife Jill were strong and kind and neither young nor old. They loved each other, and they worked hard; they liked living by the river and seeing all kinds of people from all kinds of places pass by their house. Their only sorrow was that they had no children.

After dinner, he gave them the one gift that he had to give, even though it meant giving also time when he might have been looking for Roger. He played his harp and sang for them. He sang "Sumer is i-cumen in," and "Merrily sing the monks of Ely," and then he sang the beautiful Latin hymn that he had learned at St. Alban's, "Stabat Mater."

After that people came calling for the ferry. So Adam kissed Jill good-bye and thanked her, patted the old hound once more, and crossed the river with John. The last thing Jill said to him, calling out from where she stood among the sunflowers, was: "You'll find your father! But if you don't, come back here!"

He wanted to give John one of the silver pennies left in his purse for putting him over the river, but the ferryman would not take it. "No, no, boy, keep your penny," said John, affectionately pulling Adam's cap down over his nose. "Come back to us soon and bring your father and your dog with you. That's a plucky lad," he added to a passenger with a chuckle. "Jumps into the river after his dog and swims it with all his clothes on."

Adam planned as he walked briskly back along the path to Guildford just how he would find Roger. Probably they would simply run into each other in the High Street.

"Well! Where have you been!"

"Looking for you! Where have *you* been!"

Then they would set out for Farnham and Nick, and along the road Adam would tell Roger all about John Ferryman and Jill and how good they had been to him. When they found Nick they would go back to the little house by the river and Nick would do all his tricks and Roger would tell his best tales to John and Jill. Which would they like the most? Adam thought that they would like the one about Sir Cleges and the cherries, because Sir Cleges was so kind to everyone, and then when he was in need himself, he thanked God for all His past goodness instead of asking for more, and God wrought a miracle for him. Yes, Jill would like that story. And so would John, because it had some funny parts too.

So, with his mind racing along as fast as his feet, Adam came soon to the High Street in Guildford.

Today was market day, and all Guildford was full of countryfolk who had brought their cheese and butter and vegetables and bacon and chickens to sell in town and who wanted to take home town-made things for their houses. How could you find anyone in a crowd like this? Adam squeezed through the press and made his way up the steep High Street and down Quarry Street, and in and out of all the lanes between. Churchyards and innyards, marketplace and shops: He did not miss one of them, and nowhere did he see anybody who even looked like Roger.

All the time he was aware of the castle looming on its mound, with its flint and sandstone tower rising high over the city. He and Roger had spoken of looking there for Jankin. He was saving it till last, partly because he felt shy about going up to that great, important-looking place, and partly because he was beginning to be a bit frightened about Roger, and it made him feel safer to have the castle in reserve.

At suppertime, quaking a little inside, he went to the castle gatehouse and knocked at the door. The porter, a fussy sort of man with a red face, came out and began to brandish his rod and wave him away without listening to what he said.

"No place for boys! No boys wanted here!" he barked, not unkindly. "Be off with you. Get home to your supper."

Adam stood his ground. "I am a minstrel," he said firmly. "I have right of entrance anywhere. Let me pass."

"A minstrel!" the porter's eyes began to twinkle under his shaggy eyebrows. "A half-pint size like you? You'll have to prove it to me."

Adam took his harp. How thankful he was that he had it! Suppose Jill had not guarded it for him and brought it to him!

"Thus saith Alfred," he began.

"At market and at church,
  Make friends with poor and rich,
  With all men alike.
  Then will you surely be happy,
  And fare over the land —
  Wherever you will."

The porter laughed. "Trying to make friends with me, are you? Well, you're still the smallest minstrel I ever saw."

"I'm looking for my father — Roger the minstrel," said Adam. "Is he here?"

"Roger, is it? Yes, he was here last night, with a letter from his lord, but he's not here now. The sheriff is away, but the bailiff sat at the high table and had minstrelsy till midnight. Your Roger pleased him well with his tales out of France. Roger slept in the hall last night and this morning he went out early and has not been back since."

Adam's heart tumbled down into his toes. What an evening that was, with Roger telling tales till midnight! And Adam lost hunting Nick, who was even more lost! Hadn't Roger even missed them?

"Didn't he say," inquired Adam in a very small voice, "that he'd lost a dog — and me?"

"I had no talk with him myself. Come along." He drew Adam into the paved courtyard where he felt almost crushed by towering stone walls, and beckoned to a squire in a dark tunic who was crossing from one side to the other.

"Did Roger minstrel say anything last night about losing his boy?"

"Did he indeed? He was asking every man he met had he seen a boy or a red spaniel or both. He was well-nigh distracted till Sir

Henry called him to order and told him to get on with his tales."

Adam stepped forward. "I'm the boy," he said.

The squire looked down at him and laughed. "Where's the dog?" he asked.

"Where's Roger?" said Adam desperately.

Realizing that it was no laughing matter, the squire turned serious at once. "Roger's gone to Farnham. Someone brought word about noon today that the fellow that took the dog had been seen on the Farnham Road, and thinking the boy — that's you, is it? — would be close on his heels, Roger set off forthwith for Farnham."

"Over the ferry?" said Adam, wondering how they had missed each other.

"No. Over the bridge, and the Hog's Back."

"How far is it to Farnham?" asked Adam, ready to start at once.

"Oh, it's a good nine miles. You'll have to wait till tomorrow."

Adam thought of going back to Jill and John to spend the night, but if he did, he would be on the wrong road in the morning. He wanted to go to Farnham by the same road that Roger took. He stood there looking troubled, while the squire and the porter exchanged glances over his head.

"You take him into the hall and let him get some supper," said the porter, "and he can share my bed tonight. The world is overlarge for a pint-size minstrel without his father — or his dog."

It was kind of them, but Adam did not enjoy it very much. It was not a cheerful sort of castle, even though the hall was decorated with wonderful fresco paintings by Master William the Florentine. The Lord Sheriff was seldom there, and the place had a neglected and careless sort of air. Because the tower was also used as a jail, there were guards everywhere, and they made a good deal of noise clanking about and shouting to each other and reminding you that shut away behind thick walls were men who had lost their freedom.

Supper was ample, and good enough, but afterward the bailiff called on Adam for some minstrelsy, and they all laughed even before he began. They laughed again at his songs, and called for drinking songs instead.

It was kind of the porter to share his bed, but it would have been still kinder if he had not snored loudly all night long. Adam lay awake clinging to the edge of the bed so as not to take more than his share, and missing Roger more and more with every minute that crawled slowly by.

He was thankful when morning came and he could set forth in the early freshness across the bridge and up the steep road that led over the Hog's Back to Farnham.

Arrows in the King's Forest

ADAM climbed the steep hill through the woods and came out on what seemed to be the very top of the world. On one side miles of purple heather stretched away to the green lowlands beside the Thames, where the towers and spires of London itself showed like a fairy city in the misty distance; on the other side the deep forest marched to the blue line of the South Downs and the silver sea. Where he stood, bees were busy in the thyme and the blue milkwort; the fragrant breeze blew cloud shadows over his head.

After a while, as he followed the white chalk tracks southwestward toward Farnham, the road sloped downward and the distances were hidden by trees and the shoulders of hills. More people were on the road now; he scarcely knew where they came from. He asked all he met if they had seen a minstrel with a red spaniel, or a minstrel alone hunting for a boy, but none of them had.

When he came into Farnham, where three roads met, he found the little town full of people on their way to the Fair at Winchester.

Now for the first time Adam began to be really worried. Where was Roger, and how was he to find him again among so many folk, all intent on their own affairs? The road, Roger had said, was home to a minstrel, but, thought Adam, *which* road?

In and out among the people he went all afternoon, asking everywhere his well-worn question. Three he found who had seen Jankin and Nick and thought they had gone to Winchester to the Fair, but none among them all had news of Roger.

When he got hungry, he went to the inn, and there he found one of the merchants whom he had seen at Burford Bridge. The other one had been taken ill at Guildford, and this one, who was called William of Dover, had come on alone with both their servants and their packhorses, so as to have their booths set up at Winchester when the Fair began. The sick man would follow as soon as he could.

"Loss of goods may be recovered, as the old proverb says," remarked Daun William, "but loss of time ruins us. If I am not at the Fair when it opens, I have lost half my trouble."

He made room for Adam beside him at the table, and listened to his story. "Hmm," he said musingly at last, "they told you at Guildford Castle that Roger had heard you were gone to Farnham and had set forth after you?"

"That's how the squire said it was," repeated Adam.

"Meanwhile, you had gone back to Guildford. Probably you were crossing the ferry while he was striding over the bridge! Very well, now, let's figure it out. He comes to Farnham. That would be yesterday. He finds out that Jankin has gone on to Winchester with the dog. He thinks you are close on their heels, and so he doesn't stay in

Farnham, he keeps right on toward Winchester. Isn't that it?"

That sounded reasonable, Adam admitted, although it was just as likely that when Roger had not found Adam at Farnham he might have gone back to Guildford by the other road, the one past John Ferryman's house. But Daun William seemed so positive, so satisfied with his picture of what had happened that Adam did not like to question it. After all, he was only a little boy, and the merchant was grown-up and rich and wise.

Daun William had another cup of hot spiced wine while Adam scraped his bowl of pottage. He was hungry still, for he had had only an apple and a piece of bread for dinner.

"Now I have a boy at home," said the merchant, washing his hands daintily in the bowl of water that his servant held for him. "Six years old he is, and a chip off the old block. His mother tries to make a baby of him, but he will have none of it."

A boy of six *was* a baby, thought Adam. Why, when *he* was six! He could remember the little stone house away in the north, and the music coming from the minster, and his gentle mother, who taught him to read and to sing before she died. When he was six, he used to sit on her lap sometimes, and rest his head on her shoulder, and look into the fire while she told him in her soft clear voice how he would one day be a minstrel and go on the road with his father. He had been very young when he was six.

"I wouldn't like to see him drifting about alone," the merchant was saying. "Now your father's as good a minstrel as ever I met and he had a fine letter from Sir Edmund de Lisle. I know how he'd feel about you wandering about by yourself. I tell you what! You don't weigh much. You can ride behind my man Oswald on his horse, and no doubt we'll overtake your father before we know it."

Last night at Guildford Castle, the night before at the Ferryman's house, tonight at Farnham Inn under the merchant's care! Adam thought he knew now why Roger said the road was home to the minstrel. It was because people were kind.

He was a long time getting to sleep, because he kept thinking of Roger and wondering where he was and how soon they would find each other. He was missing Nick too. If only he could have that warm silky little dog to snuggle up against, he could sleep, he thought. Was Jankin being good to Nick, and giving him plenty to eat?

In the morning Adam paid a penny out of the five still in his purse for his supper and half a penny out for his half of the bed, and he told the innkeeper what his name was and where he was going in case Roger came looking for him.

They took the road out of Farnham that went through the king's forest of Holt, beside a branch of the river Wey. They rode along close together, Daun William first, then the other merchant's servant leading a packhorse with bulging saddle-bags, then Daun William's man Oswald, with Adam perched behind him, and a laden pack-horse following them. It was not a swift progress, but it was pleasant to be riding again, though Oswald's tired and skinny horse was very different from Bayard.

It was a little mysterious to ride through the king's forest, where the trees, oak and ash and elm and beech, grew so tall, and the undergrowth was thick with fern and briar. Now and then they saw the river shining in the sunshine; now and then they saw one of the king's fallow deer standing motionless and startled in the sun-splotched shade. The birds kept their late August silence, but sometimes there was a bit of yellow and gray flitting among the leaves or a flash of wings across the road. Most of the time Adam saw only the trees that came up close to the road's edge — not cut back two hundred feet on each side as the law decreed — and heard only the steady plop-plop of their own horses' hooves. It made him drowsy after a while.

Suddenly there was a shout, and an arrow came zinging in front of them to bury its head in a tree not three feet away from Daun William. The next moment an arrow zinged behind Adam and stuck quivering in the tree nearest him. Daun William's horse, the most spirited of the five, promptly reared up on his hind legs, while the others plunged and backed against each other in fright and confusion. Amid a great crashing in the undergrowth, four men rode shouting out of the woods.

"Robbers!" thought Adam. "Robbers. This is happening to *me*."

One, the leader, wore full armor. From head to toe he was encased in chain mail that caught the sun and gave it back in a hundred winking bits. He was a knight — that Adam knew from his spurs and the crest on his helm — but he had gone to some pains to conceal his armorial bearings. His horse had no trappings; his own surcoat was plain black; even his shield had been painted over with black. Only his crest betrayed him: a gilded leopard that reared itself from the top of his steel helm. Perkin would know, thought Adam, what family bore a leopard on its crest. He had a sword with a jeweled pommel that caught the sunshine, and he carried a lance leveled menacingly at the surprised and shocked merchant.

One of the others with him was a squire, with sword and buckler, and a dagger in his belt. The other two were yeomen in green with a long bow and a quiverful of peacock-tipped arrows apiece. The knight's visor was closed and nothing of his face was to be seen, but these three others had hard, leathery faces with small, mean eyes.

Daun William had a sword, but he was too busy persuading his horse to return its forefeet to the ground even to unsheathe it. Each of his servants had a long knife at his belt, but what were two slightly dull knives against such an assortment of lances, swords, daggers, and arrows, all very sharp and plainly intended for use?

Adam peeped cautiously over Oswald's shoulder and wondered what was going to happen next.

"This is an outrage!" burst out the merchant angrily. "Sir knight, whoever you are, call off your men and let us go on our way."

The knight made no answer. The eyes of everybody almost unwillingly turned to the two packhorses and their very large, very bulging, very heavy saddlebags crammed with goods to be sold at Giles's Fair in Winchester.

The knight nodded, and the squire without a word yanked off the merchant's sword and threw it clattering to the ground, tied his hands behind him and handed the reins of his horse to one of the yeomen to hold.

"Help!" bellowed the merchant with a burst of noise that amazed Adam. "Help! Ho! Robbers! Ho!"

The servants took it up, and for a moment the woods echoed with their clamor. They made so much noise that Adam more than half expected a troop of horsemen to come galloping to their rescue. Nothing of the kind happened. The robber knight and his men silenced the other three speedily and none too gently by stuffing their mouths with their own hoods. Adam, just before they reached him, steadied himself with his hand on Oswald's shoulder, and, stretching out his neck like a rooster, screeched a final, "Help! Robbers! Ho!"

In that instant it occurred to Adam that he was still free. He slid down from the horse, bent low, and ran under his belly. A man lunged at him and grabbed his harp. With a quick twist Adam slid the thong off his shoulder. He stuck out his foot, hooked it around the man's ankle and jerked. When he felt the man topple and heard him fall, Adam turned and plunged headlong into the underbrush. Briers tore at his clothes and bushes scraped his cap off. Shielding his face with his arm, he bent over and ran close to the ground as fast as he could put one foot before the other, plowing through the thick leafy growth and dodging around trees.

He heard shouts behind him. An arrow sang over his head. He doubled back, tripped over a root, and saw as he fell a beech tree arching its branches like a green tent above his head. The next second he was up again, thinking with his feet and hands, with his knees and elbows. Before his mind had caught up, he was climbing into that beech tree, swiftly, silently, like a cat, up into the sun-mottled tangle of leaves and branches. Just as he stretched himself out flat on a big limb, he saw a piece of dead wood that had lodged in a cleft. He seized it, and flung it out into the air to fall with a snap and a rustle into the bushes twenty feet away. In that moment one of the yeomen, following close on Adam's trail, stopped short and, without looking up, turned in the direction of the noise he had heard and the ferns he saw stirring suspiciously.

Adam lay on his branch with his hot cheek against the smooth warm wood and panted softly. An ant, its pathway blocked, ran over his face and he blew it off, but silently. The loudest sound in the world just then, he thought, was the noise of his own beating heart.

The leaves, which were thick enough to hide him, also kept him from seeing what was happening. He heard footsteps as the two yeomen hunted for him, footsteps crashing nearer, then going away again, then returning right to his tree. He thought he was surely lost now, but the man had only come to get his arrow. "The boy must have gone to earth like a fox," Adam heard him call.

Presently Adam heard the sound of horses' hooves. He raised his head and strained his ears to listen. They were departing at a walk, all of them, the riders and the led horses.

Now there was silence in the wood again, except for a squirrel chattering. Adam sat up astride his limb. His face was red and throbbing, and streaming with perspiration. He wiped it with his sleeve, pushed his hair off his hot wet forehead, and slowly swung himself down from the tree. Now that the danger was over, he discovered what that scramble had cost him, where his clothes were torn and where his flesh, how his shoulder ached and his knee bled.

The road, when he limped out onto it again, bore record of the struggle in a mass of hoofprints and scattered leaves and twigs. Daun William's sword, badly rusted, lay broken on the ground. The scabbard, which had been a pretty thing, was gone.

On the other side of the road a path went into a forest. Here were more footprints. This must be the way he had taken them, that black robber knight. Adam stood and looked up that path to where it curved and vanished. Determination rose slowly like a tide within him, and set his wide mouth in a straight line.

Robbers. Stopping a good merchant who was going about his business without harming anybody! A knight, who had vowed to be chivalrous and protect the weak! Somebody ought to go after him. The sheriff or the bailiff or somebody. Besides, they had *his* harp.

With a wag of his head Adam set off resolutely down the road to find the sheriff.

Adam to the Rescue

THE sound of horses' hooves behind him made him scramble off the road again to hide behind a big clump of ferns in the ditch. When he saw that it was only a couple of chapmen with their small trunks fastened behind their saddles, he jumped out and called to them: "Hi! Stop! There's been a robbery and I want to find the sheriff!"

At the word robbery they turned pale, whipped up their horses, and galloped away, leaving Adam standing in the road looking indignantly after them.

After that Adam saw nobody till he left the wood behind. Then the first person whom he came on was a young shepherd, who was eating his dinner under a hedge with his dog sitting up watchfully beside him and his flock grazing in the field before him. Because Adam spoke the northern dialect and the shepherd an extreme southern one, they had trouble at first in understanding each other. The shepherd thought that Adam wanted something to eat and offered him some bread and salt herring.

Adam sat down cross-legged on the ground beside the strong young man with the kindly brown eyes, and had first a drink of clear cold water from the stone jug, then, a little hesitantly, some of the fish and bread. There seemed to be plenty of it, and he was very hungry. Between mouthfuls, gesticulating with his hands and going back to find other expressions for words the shepherd did not understand, he told his story.

"I want to find the sheriff," he finished. "If we go back quickly enough, maybe we can catch the robber knight and rescue poor Daun William so he can take his things to the Fair after all."

"I don't know where the sheriff is," answered the shepherd. "But Sir Adam Gurdon is bailiff. He'll be your man. He's hot against robbers. His father was an outlaw knight himself — almost thirty years ago it were, my grandam told me — and he frightened all the countryside from Farnham to Alresford. Then the king — but he was the Lord Prince then — challenged him to single combat, and they fought each other to a standstill. Prince Edward had a band of men with him, but he wouldn't let them help. So he and old Sir Adam shook hands and Prince Edward became king and made old Sir Adam bailiff of Alton. And now his son, young Sir Adam, is bailiff after him, and keeps the country clear of robbers."

"My name is Adam too."

The shepherd made a joke. His eyes crinkled first, and then his mouth twisted at the corners. "Look out for apples!" he said, and burst out laughing.

Adam smiled politely, though the joke was no new one to him. "Adam father of us all" the boys used to call him at St. Alban's, and it was considered endlessly funny to offer him an apple.

"It's the forest that gives them a chance to get away," said the shepherd, returning to the robbers. "You say he was a knight. Did you notice his bearings?"

"He'd hid them all, except his crest. That was a leopard."

The shepherd shook his head. "Sir Adam will know. He's lord of the manor here. This is his demesne land and his flock, and I'm his shepherd. The village over yonder belongs to him. You'll see the manor house beyond the church. Go tell him what you saw, and don't let the steward put you off. It's harvest time, and he'll be in a tizzy over it."

Adam thanked the shepherd for his dinner and got up to go. "Have you seen a minstrel pass this way?" he asked.

"There's many a minstrel passes this way. I don't pay much heed to them. A lass in the village told me there was one by with a dog that could walk on his hind legs like a little man — "

"When was that?" Adam interrupted eagerly.

"I don't remember. Two, three days ago."

"Was it a red spaniel?"

"Bless you, lad, I didn't see him. The lass said she wished she had one like him, but I gave her a kitten instead — pure white it were, with blue eyes and one black paw. Eh, she was pleased. Liked it better than a dog, she said."

Just like a girl, thought Adam coldly. Two-three days ago Jankin and Nick had passed this way, and some ~irl would rather have a kitten than Nick!

The wind blew softly over the field and stirred the bracken around a rock. A bird perched on a sheep's back to look for ticks, and the sheep went on cropping the short grass without noticing it. Adam felt drowsy after his dinner, and this would have been a good place to lie down and sleep for a while, but he had tarried too long already. He set off at a brisk pace in the direction the shepherd showed to him.

He passed the fields that were being harvested and saw what must have been the whole village, men, women, and children, out working in the sun. Some cut the grain with long scythes; some followed behind and bound it into sheaves; some piled the sheaves into great wagons. Franklins with rods in their hands walked among them seeing that they were doing the job thoroughly and that all of the grain went into the wagons. It was the lord's fields they were harvesting now, putting in the days of "boon work" that each villein was required to give to his lord. Across the road Adam saw the fields that belonged to the villeins waiting to be harvested. They were laid out in strips, with unplowed land between them to separate one man's holdings from another's. The breeze sweeping over the golden grain made paths and swirls in it.

The village itself was deserted, except for a few mothers and babies and lame folk. The houses and the cottages, each in its garden, clustered together along both sides of the road, while the fields and the meadows and the pastureland and woodland spread out all around them as far as the eye could see. Beyond the church, as the shepherd said, was the lord's gateway, and beyond that, sitting on a bit of a hill where it could overlook the village and the land that belonged to it, was the manor house.

It was not easy for a boy with torn clothes and no cap to convince the lord's servants, in the height of the busy harvest season, that he had important business with the lord of the manor. Without his harp Adam could not even claim a minstrel's right of entrance.

Determinedly, he stood his ground with each one he met, with porter and with usher and with steward, and he found that if he repeated the words "robber knight" often enough and clearly enough he did eventually get passed on from one man to the next in order.

It was midafternoon and the church bells were ringing for evensong before he finally won through to Sir Adam, who was in his counting room conferring with his reeve about the harvest. The reeve had a notched tally-stick, on which he was figuring this year's yield, and the knight had a parchment roll on which was written last year's score, and between the two they were growing each minute more mixed-up and cross.

"Well, what is it, boy?" snapped Sir Adam. He was a powerfully built young man, much less handsome than his own shepherd, but with the habit of authority.

"Please, Sir Knight, are you the bailiff?" said Adam respectfully.

"Yes," answered the knight. "I am. What then?"

"Can you catch robbers and put them in a dungeon?"

"Yes," Sir Adam smiled, as if he had not quite meant to, "I can. Have you got some robbers?"

"Yes," said Adam, copying the knight's style, which he admired, "I have. At least, we can get them if you hurry. They're up the

Farnham Road in the forest. They took Daun William of Dover and his packhorses and his servants, but I got away. There were five of them, and the leader is a knight. He has painted over the charge on his shield, but his crest is a leopard."

Sir Adam and his reeve exchanged looks. Both stiffened to attention.

"What did I tell you?" said Sir Adam to the reeve. "That's de Rideware without a doubt. I've suspected him this long time. You're sure of the crest, boy?"

"A leopard rampant," repeated Adam firmly.

Sir Adam began to snap out orders. "Call Walter. Tell him to bring my hauberk and sword. Have Gerald get horses. You go yourself and collect me men with crossbows. We ride at once."

The manor house, which had been sleepy in the afternoon sunshine, began to ring with the sound of running feet, of quick commands, and clattering metal. Sir Adam's squire of the body brought his coat of chain mail and helm, his shield and sword and spurs. His squire of the stable brought his horse, with trappings on which were blazoned, as on his surcoat and shield, the Gurdon arms. No hiding of his bearings for Sir Adam! From all directions men came running, some with long bows and some with the more powerful crossbows.

In an amazingly short time a band of men was ready to ride out. At its head was Sir Adam, and beside him — oh, wonder and joy! — was Adam son of Roger, on a brown palfrey to show him the way. Behind them were several squires, and the reeve, and then the archers. As they rode through the village, the people, home from the fields, crowded to the roadside to watch them pass and several of the young men ran for their bows and followed on foot.

Adam rode along in a state of high glory, wishing with all his heart that Roger could see him now, that Hugh and Godfrey could see him, and Perkin, and Jill and John Ferryman! He watched for his friend the shepherd as they went by the pasture, and made up for all the others who were not there by standing up in his stirrups and waving violently to the shepherd.

Into the forest they rode, and everyone whom they met stepped off the road into the ditch to let them pass. It took much less time to get back to the place where the robbers had jumped out of ambush than it had taken Adam to go from there to the village.

"We're almost there," said Adam. "Look, that's the tree where I hid — over there — and now you can see where the road is all cut up with hoofprints, and there's where they went into the wood."

Without pausing, Sir Adam turned into the path. "Fall back, boy," he ordered, "and ride in the midst of the men. You're too exposed here."

Adam regretfully fell back. Still, he comforted himself, he was lucky to be here at all. He told the squires about Roger and Jankin and Nick, and how he lost his harp.

"We'll get it back for you," said one, "and then you can show us what kind of minstrel you are."

The path led deeper and deeper into the forest. Sometimes they had to bend over to keep from being scraped off their horses by boughs of trees. They rode silently. Even Adam stopped chattering after a while, and felt his heart beating faster. Any minute, he thought uncomfortably, an arrow might zing through the air before his nose, or nearer.

They came to a park where the trees were sparser and the ground beneath them was cleared of undergrowth. A whole herd of fallow deer moved calmly here, scarcely even troubling to look up when the silent band of men rode past. Then the path forked, and Sir Adam took the left-hand branch. The squires nodded to one another. "He knows," said one. "He's been looking for a chance to catch de Rideware."

Before long they came to Rideware Hall, a stout stone house protected by a wall and a moat. Adam hardly knew what he expected when he saw the moat: a siege possibly, certainly a fight, and perhaps even hot lead pouring down from the top of the wall. What happened was that they found an ordinary plank bridge — not a drawbridge at all — across a stagnant and scummy bit of water shallow enough to wade. Sir Adam rode over and pounded on the door in the wall with his mailed fist.

After some delay it was opened by an agitated-looking porter.

"Sir Robert is not at home," he declared over and over, but the bailiff only pushed him aside, and the others crowded after him.

When Squire Walter leaned forward and said something in a low voice, Sir Adam, turning in his saddle, commanded: "Surround the house. There may be a postern door."

Adam heard some of the men behind him obediently wheel their horses, but his eyes and ears were all for what was going on in front of him. They were in a muddy courtyard now, where various wooden sheds were built against the thick outside wall. Some chickens fled squawking with spread wings before them, and from a pen in one corner came the excited barking of several dogs. A monkey tied to a post scrambled up it and chattered shrilly from the top. The hall itself was a stone building jutting out from the wall opposite the entrance, with narrow pointed windows, and a rather impressive flight of stone steps leading to a stout wooden door banded with iron hinges ending in a fleur-de-lis design. This door now opened, and a pale, thin lady in a green gown with wide sleeves stood at the top of the steps.

"Sir Robert is away," said she in a thin, reedy voice. "If he were here, he would resent this intrusion."

Her words were disdainful, but she looked frightened and sad. Adam felt sorry for her, and so, evidently, did Sir Adam, for he answered her gently enough as he dismounted and strode up the steps, "I have reason to believe that he is here. I must ask you to stand aside and let me enter."

His squires followed him with their hands on their swords, and after them, alternately craning his neck to look over shoulders and ducking his head to look under elbows, went Adam. Lady de Rideware gave way without further argument, and they all marched unchallenged into the hall.

It was dark inside, for the wooden shutters had been closed. The first thing was to get them open. In the light that came bit by bit, Adam saw a long room with rough stone walls. The hearth was in the center, heaped with cold ashes and half-burned logs. Down both sides ran rough board tables and benches, and at the sight of these Adam drew in his breath. They were strewn with heaps of beautiful brocades and velvets and silks, and with little bags and boxes of rare spices. In that gray, chilly, musty hall the brilliant scarlets and blues and golds of the merchant's wares made a rare show of color, and the rich fragrance of the spices rose above the dank smell of the dirty rushes on the floor. On the benches, bound and gagged, sat the merchant of Dover and his two servants, showing in their eyes and joyful squirmings their sudden relief from fright and anger.

Confusion followed. Sir Adam ran up the stairs at one end of the hall to the solar above, looking for the missing knight; others searched in the chamber below, and in the buttery and the cellar. In the excitement of the search, they forgot to free the prisoners, who beat on the floor with their feet and uttered muffled squeals to call attention to themselves. Adam took his own knife out of his wallet and with some difficulty managed to hack away the bonds first of the merchant and then of the two servants.

"He escaped through the postern when he heard you coming," cried Daun William. "Don't waste time looking for him here."

At the same moment a shout from outside drew everyone to the windows.

"They've found his trail," shouted Sir Adam. "Walter, you and Hubert stay here and see the merchant and his goods safely out on the road again. Keep Rauf and Harry with you, in case of trouble. Simon! Gerald! The rest of you! With me!"

Stamping and clanking, they were gone. The clatter of horses' hoofs in the courtyard was followed by shouts and the thudding of hooves on the grass on the other side of the moat. Walter and Hubert, the squires, and Rauf and Harry, the yeomen, watched from the windows with undisguised disappointment the departure of the rest of the band without them.

"They'll get him this time," said Walter, turning away at last. "Caught red-handed. He'd better run if he wants to keep his head on his shoulders."

Lady de Rideware had vanished. Daun William and his men were folding up the goods and repacking the saddlebags, groaning over the silks mussed and the spices spilt. It would be at best a lengthy process to get all those things back again into the proper bags in the proper order, and Daun William's nerves were in no condition to make short work of it. He fussed over the folding and refolding of each piece; he changed his mind three times about the particular box of spice and length of velvet that he would give to Sir Adam as a thank-offering. The squires tried to hurry him up, but soon, seeing that they only made him more nervous and therefore slower than ever, they gave it up and amused themselves by practicing with Rauf's crossbow, using the shabby canopy over the knight's seat at the high table as a target.

Adam prowled about looking for his harp

which he found at last among the rushes under a table. Except for a piece chipped off one corner, it was unharmed. He tuned it lovingly and plucked the strings.

"It's a lucky thing there's a moon tonight," said Squire Hubert, casting a resentful glance at the merchant who, standing in a long ray of late sunshine, still folded and unfolded and refolded lengths of material, "or we'd never get home. I wonder if they've caught de Rideware yet."

"They'll come back this way when they do, surely," said Walter. "Since we aren't with them we may as well be here as anywhere. What songs do you know, boy?"

Adam perched on one end of the table, and swinging his legs in time to the music, he harped and sang:

"Trolly, lolly, lolly, lo,
  Sing trolly, lolly, lo,
  My love is to the green wood gone,
  Now after will I go,
  Sing trolly, lolly, lolly, lo."

It was a catchy tune that Roger had taught him. They took it up, the two young squires and the yeomen. On the second round, Adam changed it:

"The robber knight's to the green
  wood gone,
    Now after we will go."

To their surprise Daun William joined in with,

"Sing trolly, lolly, lolly, lo."

The packing was finished.
"Sing trolly, lolly, lolly lo," squeaked Oswald, three bars behind everyone else.

St. Giles's Fair

ADAM rode all the way to Winchester with Daun William. The first day after the robbery and the rescue they glowed with affection for each other. Daun William said over and over that Adam was a fine brave lad who had saved him money and time and trouble and perhaps his life; he said he hoped that his own son would grow into just such a boy and that he was going to do great things for Adam.

Adam thought Daun William was a very prince of merchants, who was going to find Roger and Nick and give him a new surcoat of silk from Italy and some pennies to jingle in his purse. He was glad and proud that he had been able to help Daun William out of his troubles. He felt considerably bigger than usual, and he waggled his head as he rode along, planning — and sometimes saying out loud — just how he would describe the robbers to Roger.

The second day, however, as they made their way down the valley of the Itchen River along roads increasingly crowded with people going to the Fair, they both suffered a slight reaction. Daun William's mind was on the Fair and the difficulties of managing without his partner. He fretted over the dangers and expenses of a merchant's life and the small profit that he got for all his trouble. Adam talked about how he had tripped up the robber and hidden in the tree, how he had insisted on seeing Sir Adam Gurdon, until, with his keen sense of audience, he suddenly perceived that Daun William and the servants were all thoroughly weary of his theme. He realized that Roger would say he had been bragging. Suddenly he felt very much smaller than usual, and hollow. It came rushing over him that he had lost Nick, that he did not know where Roger was, and that Winchester was a big city.

In silence they passed the great stone buildings of Hyde Abbey and entered Winchester by the north gate.

Within the city walls was a great mass of streets and buildings, crowded and noisy and confusing. Daun William went straight to the largest inn on Cheap Street, not far from the castle and the west gate. They found the inn jammed with merchants, and the innkeeper dashing about distractedly with a saucepan in his hand and his forehead shiny with perspiration.

"It's very late in the day, sir, and we're all filled up," he exclaimed. "There's one place left in a bed with two others — very quiet gentlemen they are too, sir. That's the best I can do for you. I haven't a corner for the boy."

The servants were easily disposed of, for they would have to sit up all night and guard the packs of goods, but where was Adam to sleep? Daun William looked at him in perplexity for a long moment, and then his face suddenly cleared.

"I've got it, lad," he said. "You'll have your supper here with me, and then you'd best go to the Strangers' Hall. The good monks of St. Swithin's built it to lodge poor pilgrims, and they won't question a young lad too closely. You can sleep snugly there tonight — and perhaps you might even find your father there. In fact, I think it quite likely you will. It's one of the first places to look. But if you don't find him, then you can come to me tomorrow and I'll see what I can do. Now, that's all settled. Let's have something to eat."

Daun William ordered for Adam just what he was having for himself — and he always had the best. They had a fat partridge apiece, and mutton with a savory sauce, besides pears and gingerbread to finish with. They ate silently and both felt better when they had finished. Daun William patted Adam affectionately on the shoulder and put some pennies in his hand.

"Be sure you come to me tomorrow on Giles's Hill in the Street of Dover and tell me how you get on. Go now, before curfew rings — and sleep well."

It was important to be within doors after curfew rang. Strangers in a town were liable to be arrested on suspicion, and then, even though they were innocent of anything but being abroad after curfew, they had to stay in jail till the justices of jail delivery came to the town and heard their case. Sometimes it was six months before they were freed.

Adam thanked the merchant hastily and took leave of him.

Cheap Street on the eve of St. Giles's Fair was thronged so thick that even a slender boy like Adam had difficulty in squeezing his way through. He had no trouble in finding the Strangers' Hall, for everyone knew the way to the hall at the convent gate where the monks gave food and shelter to the poor ones among the pilgrims who came to visit the shrine of St. Swithin.

Adam found the big door standing open and walked in. A lay brother was dozing in a chair near the entrance. Adam hesitated, not sure whether he ought to wake him up and ask if he might spend the night; but the poor man looked tired, and so Adam just slipped quietly past him and went on into the long room walled with rough stone and roofed with great oak beams.

Over the fire in the center a few pilgrims were still cooking their evening meal, but most of them had already made beds for themselves on the benches along the sides of the room and had gone to sleep, their faces dim and tired in the twilight. Adam went from one to another in the big, shadowy, rustling hall, looking for Roger or for Jankin. Some did not even know he had passed, and some hunched a shoulder and rolled over impatiently, but one man in a group talking quietly under a window called out softly to him.

"Well, sonny," he said. "Looking for someone?"

"Yes, sir. I've lost my father. He's Roger the minstrel."

The man smiled and shook his head. "We're all poor men here," he said. "We've got no pennies for songs and tales. The place to look for minstrels is at the inns."

The inns! Adam had just been in the largest inn of all. He should have searched it upstairs and down, he thought despairingly. How was he ever going to find Roger if he didn't keep his wits about him any better than that?

A red-bearded man with a wide gap in his front teeth scooped up some rushes and spread his cloak over them. "Giles's Hill is where you'll find the minstrels," he said in a deep, booming voice. "Minstrels and jugglers and tumblers and all such. You'll find him in the morning. Sleep here, why don't you? It won't be so lonely."

Comforted by his friendliness, Adam curled up on the man's cloak with his wallet under his head and his harp beside him. The talk went on. Some of it he heard and some he didn't. They were countrymen from over Salisbury way, Adam gathered, all but his gap-toothed friend, who seemed to be a sailor. They were talking about King Edward.

"He loves his people, Longshanks does," said one. "And loves England. Eh, he's a good man. He's fiery in his temper, they say, but kind in his heart."

"I was on the *Magdalen* that brought the king home from France in '89," said the one Adam thought of as his friend, "and I know him as you can't know him just seeing him ride by in a procession. There's nothing in this world he fears but injustice. Knows ships and knows good seamanship. Loves a joke. Stammers a bit when he speaks, too — just like you or I might do."

"He dresses like a plain man," put in another. "That's what I like. Not all silks and embroideries and cloth of gold."

"Got all his teeth too," added the sailor who had lost his, and the others laughed.

"He hasn't been the same since the queen died," said the first one. "Eh, he loved her."

Adam sat up. "I've seen the crosses he put

up for her," he said, "wherever the casket rested on the way from York to London. There's one in St. Alban's and one between London and Westminster."

He had often passed by the one at St. Alban's without paying attention. He thought he understood a little better how the king felt, now that he had lost Roger and Nick and had to go on without them. And that was only for a little while.

"He's a great king, Longshanks," repeated the sailor. "He's strong for the law. Remember that, young fellow. He stands by the laws — and he doesn't make them all himself either."

"Who does, then?" said Adam, a little indignantly. He thought that was what the king was for.

"Parliament. There's been parliaments sitting in Winchester Castle right up the street a bit, making laws that hold the king just like they hold you and me."

A man leaning against the wall clapped his feet together impatiently and growled, "Parliament! And who goes to Parliament? The big churchmen and the nobles. Might as well be the king making the laws. Do the common people go? They do not."

"Arr. Go on. Parliaments aren't for common people. How would they get away from their work to go to Parliament?"

"Work! That's it. Common people work to get the money that keeps the king and the nobles — and the church too. 'Ever the fourth penny goes to the king,' just like the song says."

Adam was not interested in Parliaments. He hoped someday he would see the king, and Prince Edward of Carnarvon, who was just his own age. He lay down again and closed his eyes, and the voices merged into each other and faded away.

The next morning the pilgrims went to the shrine in the cathedral and then to the prior's lodging to get food and alms for their journey home. Adam returned instead to Cheap Street, from which he set out briskly for St. Giles's Hill and the Fair. He went through the east gate, passed the city mill, crossed over the river by the city bridge and followed the crowd up the hill to the Fair.

Giles's Fair was the greatest one in England, some said the greatest fair in all Europe, and it seemed this bright September morning that all England and half of Europe had come to it. He heard northern voices and midland voices and southern voices; he heard Welshmen speak; he heard Norman French and French from France; he heard tongues he had never heard before.

The Fair belonged to the Bishop of Winchester. Everybody who had a booth on Giles's Hill had to pay a tax to him, and while the Fair lasted, all the shops in all the towns for twenty miles around must be closed. The Bishop's officers went about and tested all the weights and measures to make sure that they were true; they tasted the wine and the bread that were to be sold there and threw out whatever was not of good quality. They set up a special court right in the Fair to settle any disputes that might arise — and what with all the merchants, English and foreign, and all the people who came to buy, plenty of disputes did arise. It was called the Court of the Dusty Feet, because people had come to the Fair over the roads from north and east and west, and their feet were indeed dusty, and weary too.

All of Giles's Hill was laid out in streets, each one lined with booths and tents. Every trade had its street, and every town. There were the Street of the Ironmongers and the Street of the Leatherworkers; the Street of the Welshmen and the Street of the Flemings.

Everywhere was bustle and confusion and gaiety. Up and down the streets pushed the shoppers, some intent on buying needed supplies, some just looking. Wherever two streets met or wherever there was an open space, the entertainers flocked — minstrels, jugglers, tumblers, mummers. Some wore masks, some had animals' heads on their shoulders, some led monkeys or dogs by a leash. One had a small, dusty bear that did a few clumsy dance steps.

Adam had never seen so many people or heard so much noise. He pushed through the crowd looking always for a tall man with deep-set blue eyes, looking for a red spaniel with long silky ears and a busy tail. The shouts of people beat about his head.

"Here you are, folks, needles and pins. Take home a needle to your wife and let her mend your clothes for you. Buy a pin and fix them yourself to last till you get home. Needles and pins. You over there with the red hair and the torn coat — you need some of what I've got."

"Ginger! Figs! Raisins! Almonds! Comfits for a sweet tooth. Take a fairing to your sweeting."

"Belts!"

"Purses!"

"Gloves!"

"Gather round, lordings, and hear the tale of the fox and the wolf!"

There were hundreds of people, there were thousands of people, but no Roger.

When he got hungry Adam bought himself bread and cheese and a cup of ale, and ate them looking down at Winchester. The city lay within its walls, with the king's castle and Wolvesey Castle where the bishop lived, and a hundred church spires riding high above the acres of roofs. It looked enormous. Suppose he could not find Roger! Suppose Nick was lost to him forever! Like ice forming in sudden swift splinters over a puddle, fear jabbed Adam's heart.

He sought out the Street of Dover and found Daun William in his booth, which was a substantial one with mud walls and a thatched roof. He and his men were busy unpacking his silks and spices and displaying them on counter and shelves. The whole place smelled excitingly of cinnamon and sandalwood and new fabrics.

"Oh, it's you," said Daun William. "What luck?"

"None," said Adam, "yet."

"It may take you several days. I'll tell you what, you can sleep here in the booth at night with Oswald and Harry. They're here to guard the stuff, and there's plenty of room for you. Run away now, because I'm busy, but be sure you come back later."

It made Adam feel better to have a place to return to at night. The Strangers' Hall was all right, but the fleas had been bad.

During the next few days he searched everywhere, up and down the streets of the Fair, back and forth between Giles's Hill and Winchester. He talked to everybody who had time for him and told them all about his search.

One day when he was eating his dinner of bean pottage at one of the cook shops that had been set up at the Fair, he got into conversation with a palmer. He knew the man was a palmer because he had medals all over his coat and cap showing the shrines to which he had made pilgrimages; he even had the palm of the Holy Land on his shoulder.

"I see you've been to St. Alban's," said Adam to start things going. "And Canterbury and Walsingham. What's the one next to it?"

"St. Peter's in Rome," said the palmer in a hushed voice. "And here you see I have the shell of St. James, and the head of St. John the Baptist from Amiens."

Suddenly to Adam's astonishment he took off his cap and kissed the scallop shell sewn there. "It was at St. James that a miracle was wrought for me," he explained. "My lame leg was cured. See." He jumped up from the bench and kicked out first with one leg and then with the other to show how limber he was.

"Does St. Swithin work miracles at his shrine?" asked Adam thoughtfully — "except to make it rain for forty days?"

"Sick people have been cured there. It's said that the first tower of the church fell down when wicked William Rufus was buried beneath it. That's not strictly a miracle, but it shows there is power in the place."

"Could I get a miracle if I went to the shrine?"

The palmer turned to look at Adam, his eyes twinkling. "Well now, I don't know," he said. "After all, you didn't come here to make a pilgrimage, did you? And that's what influences the saints. The farther you go and the harder the way, the greater the merit. That's only natural. But still, it wouldn't do any harm to try."

When another day came and went with no sight and no news of Roger or Nick, Adam decided to try for a miracle. So he joined a group of pilgrims entering the Cathedral by the round-arched door in the north transept, which was the only door the pilgrims were permitted to use. The monks of St. Swithin's looked on the pilgrims who came to the shrine as noisy, pushing, untidy people, greedy for too easily earned merit, who cluttered up their beautiful church. They made them go from the north door straight to the shrine behind the High Altar, and they set up elaborate wrought-iron gates to keep them out of the rest of the church.

The shrine of St. Swithin was all gold and jewels. After Adam had put some of his silver pennies in the basin he went and knelt down before the shrine among the other pilgrims. His heart beat fast. He said his Pater Noster and Confiteor as he had been taught at St. Alban's, and then he sketched out for the saint the miracle he wanted. He had no lame leg to straighten; he did not want to be suddenly clothed in fine raiment; he did not want to be cleansed of his sins or relieved of several centuries of purgatory. What he wanted was to see Roger come striding through the crowd with Nick under his arm. Gentle St. Swithin, who taught King Alfred when he was a little boy and loved him well, surely this would be an easy and pleasant miracle for you to work!

Adam opened his eyes wide and looked for Roger. All he saw was the other pilgrims and the wrought-iron gates, and beyond them the long pillared aisles touched with color by the sunlight streaming through painted glass windows.

"The Fall of Adam"

ADAM followed the crowd. A crowd might mean a minstrel — and the minstrel might be Roger.

He was in a part of Winchester that he had not yet explored, south of the King's Gate, near St. Michael's Church. When they came to the churchyard, the group that Adam was following merged into a larger crowd and came to a halt. Adam tried to worm his way through to find out what they were looking at, but he could not, for they all stood closely together and stuck out their elbows defensively at any pressure from behind.

"What is it? What's going on?" said Adam to a man beside him.

"It's a miracle play. They've been announcing it all over the parish. We've not had one since Plow Monday." The man raised his voice. "Move a little closer up front, can't you? We can't see back here."

From the front came an angry "Sh!"

Adam tried to creep in around the edges, but the mass of people pressed up tight against the churchyard wall. It must be a good play, he thought.

He joggled the elbow of a lanky man who had brought a stool to stand on. "Please, sir, what play are they giving?" he asked in a loud whisper. He had seen the Resurrection Play performed in the marketplace at St. Alban's at Easter time, and that had been wonderful.

"It's *The Fall of Adam*," said the man. "It's already begun. See that platform? That's Paradise. They've got it rigged up for fair this time."

"Sh!" said somebody.

So it was *The Fall of Adam*, was it! All the more reason why Adam Quartermayne ought to see it! And by hook or crook he would.

An idea struck him. He turned and ran out through the churchyard gate and along the wall outside till he came to the place where it met the church itself, at a right angle. It was high and offered fewer footholds than the abbey wall at St. Alban's had done — he thought of Perkin and wished that he were there too — but by using the church to brace knees and elbows against, he managed with a heave and a puff and a scraping to get himself up. Then he ran along the top till he found the spot from which he had the best view, and sat down with his legs dangling over into the churchyard.

Below him on the right was the audience; rising above him on the left was the old stone church; directly in front, and a little below the level of his eyes was the platform rigged up to represent Paradise. It was hung with curtains from about three feet above its floor all the way to the ground below, and above the curtains showed a wealth of green boughs hung with flowers and fruit. One leafless sapling stood by itself, with large green apples tied to its branches.

Above the curtains, which hid the lower part of their bodies, Adam in a scarlet tunic and Eve in a white silk gown and cloak could be seen moving about with evident enjoyment. Now and then they took a pear or a plum from one of the bushes, but they shuddered away from the apple tree.

Underneath the platform evidently was Hell, for several demons in black with black faces came running out from between the curtains. They looked up at Paradise and pointed out the forbidden apples to Eve. Adam on the wall was delighted. He wished that he were down there playing the part of one of the demons.

Then a bigger demon, with horns and tail, approached Adam in Paradise and suggested that he have an apple, which he declined with a burst of righteous indignation. The big demon joined the little demons and they all went into Hell to confer.

Now came one of the most exciting moments of the play. The audience apparently knew that it was coming for they whispered and craned their necks eagerly. Up from the bushes beside the apple tree, waving back and forth as if it were really alive, came a large and hideous serpent. He spoke to Eve in a coaxing voice that came, appropriately, from underneath the platform.

"I tell you sooth, I will not lie.
Come eat the fruit, you shall not die.
For God doth know, though he disguise,
Who eats this fruit is straightway wise,
His eyes see far and he does grow
Himself a god and all things know."

This was too much for Eve. She took an apple from the tree — untying it with some difficulty — bit it, and handed it to Adam, who ate up the rest of it.

As soon as he had thrown away the core, however, remorse set in. He ran away and hid, disappearing from the view of the audience below the curtains. But Adam Quartermayne from his high seat on the wall could see the other Adam crouched in a corner of the platform changing his scarlet tunic for a rough green one sewn together in the semblance of fig leaves.

Now from the church door a Figure in a surplice and stole came forth and mounted the steps to Paradise. Eve in her turn ran and hid — and changed her shining white silk cloak for a drab and ragged one.

It was no use their hiding. They had to come forth and stand with bowed heads before the Figure, while with fearful denunciation he drove them out of Paradise.

A sigh that was almost a groan swept the audience. Adam Quartermayne hitched himself forward on the stone wall, hoping to see more of the demons.

Slowly descending the steps from Paradise Adam carried a spade and Eve a distaff and spindle, as symbols of the work that they would now have to do to earn their bread. Adam delved in the ground with the spade and Eve spun, and both wept and groaned, stopping now and then to point longingly up at Paradise, while demons ran out from under the platform and planted thorns and thistles in the earth where Adam was digging.

As if that were not enough, more devils came forth and hung clanking iron chains on the necks of Adam and Eve. With horrible grimaces and loud shouting and booing they dragged the poor sinners off to Hell and pushed them in through the curtains. The demons outside did a dance of triumph and the demons inside set up a great clashing of pots and kettles. Adam on the wall leaned over to see better.

Finally just when the din was at its most terrific, actual smoke gushed out from between the curtains.

At this culmination of realism, Adam Quartermayne fell off the wall.

Adam Meets Some Minstrels

WHEN he came to, he was lying in a bed with linen sheets and a soft coverlet. He raised his head to see more of his surroundings, but immediately the whole room turned upside down with such a sick, hot swirl that he put his head hastily back on the pillow again and closed his eyes.

His head hurt. Cautiously he lifted his hand to his forehead and felt there a soft linen bandage.

Gradually the dizziness passed and he ventured to open his eyes again. This time he saw without moving his head that he was in a little room with painted canvas on the walls and a narrow window, beyond which was a garden and an apple tree. The sight of the apple tree brought back to his memory Adam and Eve and Paradise and the demons. Why, he must have fallen off the wall!

Then who had brought him here and undressed him without his knowing it, and laid him in this soft, smooth bed? And where were his clothes and his harp? When he tried to look for his harp, the dizziness came again.

Sometime later he heard footsteps and low voices. The door opened slowly, and he saw two faces peering in, one above the other. The lower one was a small, plain feminine face, with a turned-up nose and a round little folded-over chin, not young, but still childlike; the other was a man's face, with clearcut features, that wore an expression of remote serenity.

"He's awake," whispered the woman, and they both tiptoed into the room and stood beside the bed looking down at Adam without speaking.

"Please," said Adam, "where is my harp?"

"It's hanging on the peg over yonder," said the man.

Adam lifted his head to see and the dizziness swooped again. While he waited with tight-closed eyes for it to clear he tried to think where he had heard that voice before, low and clear and full of authority. Then he remembered that it was the voice of the Figure in the play, and opening his eyes again he saw that the man wore the black gown and cap of a parish priest. So that was how he got here!

The woman, who wore a wimple and a dark gown, had a bowl and spoon in her hand. Drawing up a stool close to the bed, she sat down and began to talk.

"Now you shouldn't have been climbing on the churchyard wall," she said, "but you did, and you hurt your head, poor boy. Can you sit up? 'No, I see you can't. Lie still and don't try again. I've got some milk and wastell bread for you, and I'll just feed it to you as if you were a baby robin."

Feeling rather silly, Adam obediently opened his mouth and she poked into it spoonfuls of the fine white bread softened in fresh milk.

"I am Master Walter, the vicar of this parish," said the priest, "and this is Dame

Prudence, my sister. What is your name, my son?"

Adam, who had just taken a large mouthful, chewed and swallowed hard; it seemed a long time before he could answer: "Adam Quartermayne, sir, Roger the minstrel's son."

Master Walter's cool brown eyes suddenly warmed with amusement. "Adam is it?" he said. "So we had the Fall of Adam in earnest as well as in play."

His sister nodded her head vigorously. "And it was a real miracle as well as a miracle play," she said, scraping the spoon noisily around the sides of the pewter bowl. "I thought the lad was done for. So he's a minstrel's son. Then *that's* why," she explained to Master Walter, "he carried a harp."

"No doubt," said Master Walter. "Where is your father, my son?"

To his annoyance Adam's eyes suddenly filled with tears. All the times he had been alone and kept from crying — and now he had to go howl like a baby! "I don't know," he answered quaveringly. "I've been hunting for him nearly three weeks. I've lost my dog too."

"Dear me. That is sad," said the priest sympathetically. "We must see what we can do to help you. The first thing is to mend your head. Lie still, and sleep awhile."

It was many days before Adam was up and about again. A broken head is no joke. He lay as patiently as he could in the fine bed, while his mind went tramping over the white tracks in the chalk downs, searching for Roger. Sometimes he longed so keenly for Nick that he could almost feel a silky head butting itself under his palm to be petted. Dame Prudence and Master Walter were endlessly kind to him. He knew that they came to love him, but he felt so much gratitude toward Dame Prudence and so much respect for Master Walter, that he was never quite comfortable with either. Dame Prudence let him have his harp on the bed with him, and Master Walter lent him a book in which, written out in a clear black hand and decorated with gold and blue and scarlet, were stories of the saints. It was all in Latin, and Adam had already forgotten most of the Latin he had learned at St. Alban's, but it pleased Master Walker so much to come in and find him reading instead of harping, that he would work away manfully at the hard words until his head ached again.

September passed and October came. The

leaves of the apple tree outside the window turned yellow, and a damp mist wrapped them round. Rain poured down, and they fell, first in flocks and then by ones and twos. When the sun came again it shone on a robin perched on a bare branch singing his autumn song.

When at length Adam could sit up without getting dizzy and the bandage was off his head, Dame Prudence brought him an armful of clothes and told him to get dressed. Adam was delighted. He scrambled into his cotte and breeches, which had been washed and neatly mended, into his hose, and his shoes which had been patched and oiled so that they were almost as good as new. When he came to his outer clothes, he stopped and frowned. Here was a surcoat of leaf-brown wool, a white coif to tie under his chin, and a hooded cloak lined with gray: good, warm garments all of them, but depressingly sober. Nobody would know he was a minstrel when he had those things on! He put them on, nevertheless, for he had nothing else, and went to find Dame Prudence and ask for his own back again.

"Now you look like a Christian," she said approvingly. "I gave your old surcoat away.

It was ragged and faded — and too gaudy anyhow."

Adam looked at her aghast. Roger had brought him his gay striped surcoat from France! What if it was ragged and faded? It was a minstrel's coat — and this, this was the costume of a parish clerk!

As if answering his thoughts, Dame Prudence went on complacently, "Our parish clerk outgrew these clothes before he wore them out. It would please Master Walter if you were to help the clerk with his duties. Then later, perhaps, when Cuthbert has gone to the university, you could take his place."

"But I'm a minstrel, not a clerk," protested Adam, "and I have to find my father."

"Yes, of course," agreed Dame Prudence brightly. "But that may take some time, and you will wish to help here as you can. Go out into the sunshine now. The color is all gone out of your cheeks and even your freckles have faded."

The garden was enclosed with a high wall. A red rose still bloomed in a sunny corner and gossamer lay on the grass like fairy washing spread out to dry. Overhead, white clouds went sailing in a deep blue sky.

Adam walked forlornly up and down the

paths and over the stake-strewn furrows of the vegetable garden, feeling weak in his knees and very low in his mind. He looked in the barn, and sniffed the fragrant hay; he stroked the long nose of a horse that hung its head over the stable door; he peered into the dairy and then into the kitchen where preparations for dinner were going forward with a great odor of fish, for it was Friday.

At dinner, Adam sat next to Cuthbert, the parish clerk.

"I'm to help you," said Adam. "What do you do?"

"I take care of the church. Then at mass I carry the holy water, and sometimes read the epistles and responses. Master Walter has been teaching me, and when I'm old enough I'm going to take orders. Sometimes when Master Walter goes to visit the sick I follow him with bell and candle."

"I could do that," said Adam, cheering up a little. It sounded rather like a procession. "And if they have any more miracle plays I could be a demon."

"You'd better sweep the floor and polish the candlesticks," said Cuthbert.

"I could do that," agreed Adam with a

sigh, "in the mornings, and then go looking for Roger the rest of the day."

Besides Master Walter and Dame Prudence and Cuthbert, an old man was there for dinner who had come with a message from the hospital at St. Cross. When they had all finished eating, Adam unslung his harp from his shoulder. He would do whatever they wanted him to do, to show his gratitude, but he would also give his own gift of song and story.

"Would you like some minstrelsy?" he said. Taking the silence in the room for acceptance, he plucked his harp strings and sang, as persuasively as he knew how, the song of the Irish minstrel:

"I am of Irelande,
   And of the holy lande,
      Of Irelande.
   Good sir, pray I thee
   For of saint charity
   Come and dance with me
      In Irelande."

That, he thought, ought to get them into the spirit of it.

"The boy has a beautiful voice," said Master Walter. "Such a voice is a gift of God and should be used in God's service."

"Isn't it God's service to make people merry?" asked Adam. Master Walter cleared his throat, but the parish clerk answered first. "No," he said flatly.

Adam sang the cuckoo song next.

"The monks of Reading," said Dame Prudence, "have put better words to that tune — holy words."

Master Walter sat with his elbow on the table and his hand shielding his eyes, in a thoughtful way he had; Dame Prudence had taken up her distaff and spindle and was busy twisting wool into yarn; the parish clerk looked at the ceiling; but the old man from St. Cross slapped his knee with delight.

"D'you know 'My love is to the greenwood gone'?" he exclaimed. "Sing that, boy. Sing that." Then he looked around the silent room, and his expression changed. "Meaning no offense," he mumbled.

Perhaps a tale would be better. Adam tried to think which one would be most appropriate. "Remember," Roger used to say, "a minstrel's first duty is to suit his listeners. Minstrels have a bad name with church folk. And why? Because of the tales they have told them. 'Emma and the Plowshares' is the tale I sang at the enthroning of the Abbot John of Waverly, and that was well liked."

"Listen, lordings," said Adam, beginning as he had often heard Roger begin, "and I will tell you how the holy Queen Emma walked on red-hot plowshares in Winchester Cathedral — "

Master Walter raised his hand. "Let us have no secular tales, my son," he said kindly, but very firmly. "Remember that St. Paul wrote to Timothy reproving those who lay aside truth and tell tales and fables and such poor devices. We have miracle plays in the churchyard, because some poor people have minds fit to learn Bible history only through mumming and playacting, but the vicar's household must stand for higher ways."

Adam lowered his harp. A lump in his throat prevented him from saying anything. Master Walter put a kindly hand on his head. "You shall sing in the choir," he said. "That way you can best please God — and me."

Every day after that, Adam helped Cuthbert put the church in order and polish the great candlesticks and the silver chalice. Every day he sang with the choir at matins and at evensong. And every day he went out to look for Roger and Nick.

If he didn't find them soon, he thought despairingly sometimes, he just could not stand it! He did not want to be a parish clerk. He was a minstrel.

The Fair was gone from St. Giles's Hill now, and most of the minstrels and tumblers with it, but still travelers came to the inns and Adam kept hoping that at one or another of them, or among the crowd on Cheap Street, he would find Roger looking for him.

One day at a miserable alehouse in a back alley, he met a little band of minstrels and tumblers: a man and a woman and two lads of fifteen or so. It was a raw, cold day with sudden gusts of rainy wind, and for all his warm clothes, he felt chilled to the marrow. They, in fluttering tunics thin with wear, were much more pinched than he. They hovered over the fire so closely that they were all but kneeling in the ashes. Cold, and thin, and hungry looking, they yet had an easy friendliness and a gaiety that went to Adam's heart. There was a dog too, a skinny, restless little greyhound that kept jumping about. If anyone stretched out an arm for him, he jumped over it; if not, he just jumped. After Adam patted his head and tickled him behind the ears, he sat down in front of Adam and scratched impatiently at his leg with a sharp paw if he stopped for a moment. One of the boys had a tabor, and the woman a wry-necked flute, the man a pipe. The other boy turned somersaults and walked on his hands. He was so tall and thin that it seemed as if he must break himself in two, or tie himself in knots that he could not untie.

They all performed for Adam, and Adam played on his harp and sang for them.

"You can harp," said the younger boy admiringly. "No one would ever think to look at your clothes that you were a minstrel."

"I am the son of Roger Quartermayne," said Adam proudly.

For the first time the name of Roger woke comprehension in the faces of those who heard it.

"Why — ee — " exclaimed the older boy.

"Wasn't he the fellow — " began the woman.

"Have you seen him?" cried Adam. "Where was he? How long ago? Tell me!"

"It was two — three weeks ago," said the woman, "at Giles's Fair, it was. At the Court of the Dusty Feet. Roger was there in a dispute with another minstrel — I don't remember his name. A little dark fellow."

"Did he have a red spaniel? Was his name Jankin?"

"Jankin. That was it. And it was all about this spaniel dog — the dispute. They got into a regular fight at the Fair, and got haled into court for it. Roger says the dog was his, and this Jankin swears he'd traded a horse for it. Roger says he doesn't want the horse, he wants the dog. He admits it's a good horse, but lame, though that wasn't why he didn't want it. It was all mixed up. I forget the ins and outs —"

"He said the dog belonged to his boy —" put in the thin boy.

"Yes, that was it, but he said he'd lost the boy. Everyone laughed to see a man claiming he'd been cheated because he got a war horse instead of a little spaniel dog."

"How did it come out?" persisted Adam, almost frantic with suspense. "Did he get the dog back?"

"No. Why should he?" said the man. "All the court had to go on was just what the two said. Jankin had the dog — and possession is nine points of the law. The magistrate told Roger to go on back to Burford Bridge and get his horse and think himself lucky."

"Did he go?"

"I suppose so. He had to leave Winchester. The magistrate told him there wasn't room for the two of them. How you look, boy! What's wrong?"

"Oh," cried Adam, "that was my dog Nick! And now he's lost and Roger's gone and I don't know where he is!"

"*Your* dog! How did Jankin get it if it was yours?"

Adam told them. He told them how he had followed Jankin and Nick, and how he had swum the Wey, about John Ferryman and Jill, about Daun William and the robbers and Sir Adam; and about *The Fall of Adam.* "Roger was here," he finished with a wail, "and Nick, and all the time I was in bed with a broken head."

"What we've got to do," said the woman, and Adam began to feel better right away, hearing her say *we* instead of *you,* "is try to think what Roger would be most likely to do. He'd go back to Burford Bridge and get the horse, wouldn't he?"

They all nodded.

"Then — he was Sir Edmund's man, you say. He'd be expected back at de Lisle House for Christmas, wouldn't he?"

"Yes, but he'd look for me first."

"Of course he would. But see here, he'd *been* looking, hadn't he? He'd come to Winchester and looked high and low without finding you. Now, maybe he'd think this way: He'd know you knew he'd got to go back to Sir Edmund for Christmas. He'd maybe think you'd gone to London instead of Winchester, after all, and he'd follow you there. Isn't that logical?"

They nodded again, and the man thumped his palm with his fist. "I believe you've hit it, Mother," he said. "Now I've got an idea too. We're going up to London ourselves. Why don't we start right away, and Adam here can go with us. We could use a harp all right. Can you do any tumbling, son?"

"Not with a sore head," said Adam ruefully. He had already tried it in the garden. "But I can juggle knives. Look. Lend me a knife, somebody."

He took his own out of the case in his wallet and the younger boy lent him one. He threw them up, catching one while the other was in the air, making them turn over and over and come down so that he could grasp the handles.

"That's good. That'll do fine. Well — how about it?"

To be out on the road! To be with minstrels. To be on Roger's trail again!

"Oh, yes!" he cried eagerly. "Oh, *yes!*"

"I'm Jack de Vesey and this is Alison my wife, and this lad is Lawrence and the tiny one there is Andrew."

Andrew, who was half a head taller than any of them, grinned sheepishly.

Adam thought of Dame Prudence and Master Walter. How kind they were, how good. How disappointed they were going to be in him. However could he say good-bye to them, and if he did, would they let him go? He decided to write it instead.

None of his new friends had parchment or pen; in fact, they were all highly amused at the idea that they could use either if they had it. Adam went into a shop in Cheap Street, where the shops were open again now that the Fair was over, and bought a kerchief as a parting gift for Dame Prudence. Then he got a piece of parchment and borrowed a pen and wrote her a note to go with the present. Andrew offered to leave it at the vicarage door and run right back.

It had been a bad week for the de Veseys, and none of them had any money for dinner. They had spent their last farthings for ale, as much for the chance to get warm by the fire as for the ale itself. Adam, after his purchase, had still a few pennies in his purse, and so he paid for dinner for them all. It took all the money he had, but he did not care. They were minstrels together, and they were starting even!

Early in the afternoon they went through the north gate. The sky was gray, and a cold wind ruffled the pewter-colored river and bent the grasses on its banks. The road stretched before them. Adam felt wildly excited and almost happy.

Hue and Cry

AFTER the rain and the cold, St. Martin's Summer brought a spell of warm, sunny weather. The country people were busy plowing the fields and sowing the winter wheat and rye, while rooks cawed in the trees and daws chattered and robin redbreasts flashed among the few remaining leaves. Then they drove the cattle and sheep and swine in from the fallow fields and the woods. Some they penned up for the winter, but most they sold, or slaughtered and salted for food during the cold months. By Martinmas all the outdoor work was done, the fieldfares had come flying home from over the seas to spend the winter in England, and it was time to work inside the barns, threshing the grain with long, hinged flails and winnowing it with baskets called fans or with sieves.

The people of the manner houses went hunting. Sometimes Adam and his minstrel friends would meet them with hawks on their fists. A heron would rise out of the reeds, and soon a falcon would circle swiftly to grasp it in her talons. The tinkle of the silver bells reminded Adam of Simon Talbot. He wondered where Simon was now, and if his broken heart had mended.

Once in the forest near Alresford they heard the exciting sound of a hunting horn and the baying of hounds; the next moment a roe dashed past right in front of them, and after it came the big deerhounds, their powerful muscles of thigh and shoulder rippling as they ran; behind the hounds men in bright hunting attire came riding. They were gone in a minute, but the stir of their passing hung in the air for a little while.

In mid-November the rain came again, and the cold, and the fog. The days closed in early.

It was a good time for minstrelsy, because nobody could go to sleep so early and the long evenings must be filled in somehow. When a book cost more than a horse and few could read, minstrels' tales were almost the only entertainment. Minstrels brought news too; they told what was going on in the next town, and what was happening in London, and where the king was.

If Roger had been there, he and Adam would have spent many a warm happy evening with all kinds of people at all kinds of firesides, great and simple, but the de Veseys rarely got into people's houses. They did their stunts and told their stories in the market place or on the green. Jack would talk about the revolt in Wales and King Edward's going to quell it with the aid of the barons who held land in the Welsh Marches, but when people found that he knew no more about it than everybody did, they paid no more attention to him. Sometimes the de Veseys got a few halfpence, but when dusk came and they knocked at a house door they were usually turned away. At the small houses, when they were told there was no room, there was nothing they could do. At the big houses Jack would demand a minstrel's right of entrance. "We want no jugglers and tumblers here," the porter would snap, and slam the door. They slept in barns, if they were lucky, and under hedges or haystacks if they were not. They were often hungry and cold.

Adam longed more and more for Roger. The de Veseys were jolly people and kind in their way, but they made him as uncomfortable as Master Walter and Dame Alice did, though for very different reasons.

They were always promising and never doing. "This very afternoon," they would declare, "Adam shall tell one of his tales, and tomorrow we will surely start for London." But when the afternoon came, Jack was noisily roaring out his own coarse stories and the boys turning somersaults, and Adam never had a chance to lift his voice. Instead he had to play tunes on his harp to attract attention to the others, or provide music for Andrew when he danced on his stilts. And when the next morning came they were off to Martyrs Worthy or to Chiddingford or Witley, anywhere but along the road to London.

The stories that Jack told were not at all like those that Roger used to tell. They were short, exaggerated tales mostly making rude jokes about friars and monks and rich abbots. Adam knew that friars were often greedy and untruthful, that monks sometimes varied the holy life with hunting and chess-playing and frequently ate and drank too much, that some rich abbots were as powerful and unscrupulous as many rich nobles; but who could be better than Master Walter and Dame Alice, or the monks at St. Alban's?

"People like the stories we tell," Andrew said, when Adam objected. "You have to give people what they want. You pretend to be a minstrel. You ought to know that."

At first that sounded like what Roger used to say. "A minstrel must fit his tale to his listeners," but when Adam thought it over he decided that it was quite different. Roger told tales that fitted the good in people, tales about courage and danger and adventure and love. "Well anyhow," Adam persisted, "Roger got a war horse for his tales and that's more than Jack ever did."

He was sorry the minute he said that. It was a very sore point with the de Veseys that so few farthings came their way.

"Listen, young 'un," said Andrew. "I've heard all I want to hear about Roger. Day and night you talk about him, and I've had enough. From now on, don't even say his name. Here, lend me your harp."

Andrew, who had no instrument of his own, was forever borrowing Adam's harp.

That was another thing that made Adam uneasy, and yet he did not like to refuse it.

They were resting on a bank in the Forest of Holt outside Farnham. While Andrew plonked away at the harp, Adam looked up at a holly tree over his head and wished that the berries were edible. They had had nothing to eat all day, and it was past dinnertime.

Adam told the others about what happened the last time he had been in the Forest of Holt, about the merchant and the robbers.

"Sir Robert de Rideware could come riding down this road right now," he finished, "and I wouldn't worry a bit. That's one thing about not having silks and spices — nobody wants to take anything away from you!"

"But that's how some people get silks and spices," said Lawrence gloomily, "taking them away from somebody else." A heavy black lock of hair fell down his forehead and he shook it back like a restive horse.

"Look," said Alison. "Look at that!"

Along the road came three men in shabby green with bows and arrows. Behind them was another on a black horse carrying a deer over his saddle, its legs sticking out stiffly on either side. Two boys followed leading grey-hounds coupled together, four white, two

tawny, and two red. They passed the minstrels without noticing them and a little
farther down the road they turned off on a
path leading into the forest. When they had
disappeared, Alison gasped: "They've been
hunting in the king's forest."

"I wouldn't mind having a good piece of
venison myself," said Jack with a sigh, and
Andrew rubbed his stomach and licked his
lips.

"If they get caught they'll be blinded," said
Adam.

"That's the least of what will happen to
them," said Alison vigorously. "Hunting in
the king's forest! I wouldn't want to eat
venison caught that way, no matter how
hungry I was."

"Venison's venison," said Lawrence, "and
most likely they won't get caught. Why should
the king or anybody else own miles of forest
and say that no hungry man is to shoot a
deer or a hare in it for his dinner?"

"Hush," said Alison.

"I won't hush," muttered Lawrence sulkily,
lowering his voice nevertheless. "Why should
some be hungry and others have more food
than they can eat?"

There being no answer to this question,

they got up and trudged on to Farnham. Adam, as usual, asked everyone he met if they had seen Roger the minstrel or Jankin and a red spaniel, though he had long ago given up expecting any answer but *no*, and was pinning his hopes on London and Christmas.

They had little luck in Farnham that day. They got only enough farthings for a glass of ale and a bit of bread all round, and that was not nearly enough for such hungry people. Adam felt tired and dizzy.

"Let's go to the church," he begged. "The parson will give us something to eat and maybe a bed for tonight."

"Catch a parson giving anything to a minstrel," said Jack scornfully.

"Master Walter gave food to any hungry man who came to his door," persisted Adam.

"Look at Lawrence! What's he got?"

Lawrence, who had vanished a short while ago, now joined them with a mysterious gleam in his black eyes and a big bulge in the front of his surcoat. He jerked his head imperatively and they all wonderingly followed him down the High Street and out of the town.

At the edge of a field he stopped and looked around; then he began to take things from beneath the front of his surcoat, a loaf of bread, part of a leg of mutton, and a meat pie, still warm.

"Food," he said simply.

Spread out on the frost-hard ground, without cloth or platter, it looked and smelled unbelievably good. Their hands all fluttered out toward it.

"Benedicite!" exclaimed Jack under his breath.

"Here," said Alison. "Wait till I get my knife out and I'll divide it properly."

The biggest pieces went to Jack, the next largest to Lawrence and Andrew, the smallest to herself and Adam. They ate without saying a word till the last crumb was gone. Then Jack leaned back against the trunk of a tree and sighed deeply. "Ah," he said. "I feel better."

Adam too felt warmed and cheered. The whole world took on a different look. The sky was brighter and the wind less cold. Even the skinny dog, to whom he had given part of his mutton, looked more lovable than usual.

"I could eat that much again," said Andrew.

"Gluttony is one of the seven deadly sins," Alison reproved him primly. "They represent it by a swine in the books."

Lawrence kept looking over his shoulder toward the town. Far down the road, small in the distance, some people now came running and waving their arms.

"Come on," cried Lawrence. "We've got to get out of here."

The urgency in his voice left them in no doubt. Suddenly pale, they all jumped up and set off as fast as they could go along the road toward Guildford.

Adam with his shorter legs had to trot to keep up with the others. Hurrying so soon after eating gave him a sharp pain in his side, and his head began to ache. Worst of all was the knowledge that flared in his mind like a flash of lightning and jabbed his heart with terror: Lawrence had stolen the food that they had just eaten. Adam had never been so frightened in all his life. He had never before been on the wrong side of the law.

It was nine miles to Guildford and the afternoon was already well along. Could they shake off their pursuers and get there before curfew?

Nobody said a word. They had to save their breath. Running at first, then slowing up to an easier jog-trot, they covered the distance between Farnham and Whitewaysend in an hour. There the road forked, one branch going up over the Hog's Back, the other through the forest. Jack stopped and rubbed his forehead which, in spite of the chill of the day, was wet with perspiration.

"Which way?" he said.

The road through the forest led past Jill and John Ferryman's cottage. Adam thought longingly of the haven he had found there, but he would not take a gaggle of minstrels there, all wanted for stealing a dinner. Gaggle was the wrong word, he thought, remembering Simon's teaching. A melody of harpers, you should say, or a poverty of pipers. A poverty of pipers they were, certainly. That reminded him that Andrew still had his harp. He started to ask for it, but at that moment Jack decided on the road over the Hog's Back, and they were off again.

The people from Farnham who had been following them had long ago given up and turned back. The point was now to get to Guildford before curfew.

Up and up went the white chalk tracks through the rusty brown bracken and the purple brown heather. As dusk came on, the wind grew sharper; it whistled in the bushes and whipped Adam's hair across his chapped

cheeks. There were no wide views now of the
Weald and the South Downs on one side or
the silver Thames and London towers on the
other. There was just the wind and the gray
sky, and the dark creeping out of the low
bushes at their feet. Adam's heart pounded
in his chest and his breath came in gasps.

It was quite dark when at length the road
pitched down the hill to the river. They heard
curfew ringing several minutes before they
reached the bridge.

"Now what are we going to do?" said Andrew. "I for one don't care to be picked up by
the watch and spend the next six months in
the dungeon at Guildford Castle."

"If we go in quietly we won't arouse the
watch," answered Jack. "William the glover
will let us sleep in his counting house if we
can get to him."

They slipped like shadows across the bridge
and felt their way up the steep dark High
Street. Whenever they heard a footfall or a
voice they stood stock-still and scarcely
breathed, like baby partridges freezing
among the leaves when danger approaches.
They got safely enough to William the glover's house, but waking him up was another
matter. All his windows were shuttered tight,
and his door locked.

Andrew whistled and Jack knocked, softly at first and then more loudly.

Suddenly someone shouted behind them and lantern light cut through the darkness.

"Halt where you are!" commanded a harsh voice.

The lantern was lifted so as to shine on all their white, startled faces. Adam saw the shadows flee into the sharp hollows of Lawrence's thin cheeks, making him look like some sinister bird.

"Who are you and what are you doing here?"

"We're minstrels, may it please you, sir," answered Jack with a whine in his voice that made Adam wince. "We were trying to wake William the glover to let us in to sleep."

"That's a likely story. Will went to London three months ago. A Flanders man has his shop. Minstrels, eh! Where d'you come from so late?"

"From Farnham, sir," answered Jack in the same moment that Lawrence, evidently believing that Farnham had better not be mentioned, said, "We've come from Gomshall and we lost our way in the Downs."

"From Farnham and from Gomshall, is it, and you met here in the dead of night to try

Master Etienne's windows. I say it looks suspicious and you look like suspicious characters, and I arrest you in the name of the law."

It had happened. Adam's heart sank. What would become of them? How would Roger ever find him now?

"Run!" shouted Jack. "Scatter!"

He shook the watchman's hand from his shoulder, knocked down the lantern, and kicked it. There was a little squeal from Alison, a scuffle, and the sound of running feet. Adam felt Andrew go past him in a rush before he too turned and ran, stumbling in the dark, groping with his hands to find a way between walls and fences.

Now the watchman raised a shout. It was a mighty bellow of a shout, and it meant but one thing: It meant that he was raising the hue and cry according to the statute made at Westminster in the thirteenth year of King Edward. Once before Adam had heard the hue and cry levied, but never had he imagined that he would be one of those cowering in the shadows.

In all the houses round about, shutters were thrown wide and heads thrust out. The next minute the doors opened and men with torches and lanterns came tumbling out all along the street. Each one shouted as he ran. The din spread to the next street and the next.

Now Adam's run through Guildford before, when he was following Jankin, helped him; he remembered the back lanes and the steps that led down to the river. He darted across the street and crouched behind a water barrel, until a man with a lantern had pounded past shouting "Stop! Robbers!" Then, in the lantern's faint backward gleam he made for a doorway and flattened himself against it in the shadows, while two Guildford burgesses ran headlong into each other and hung on, each convinced that he had caught a thief.

Bit by bit, in the dark, amidst all the noise and shouting, Adam groped his way to the steps and scrambled down them. When he reached the river he turned to the right and ducked under the bridge.

There he squatted on the wet gravel between the water and the stone pier, while the hue and cry spread from the town on the right side of the river to the settlement around St. Nicholas's Church on the left bank. It was bitterly cold and dank under the bridge. The stones above his head oozed moisture, and the river sent up an icy breath as it flowed past in the blackness. Adam was stiff and aching; his teeth chattered so loudly that he thought people running across the bridge above him must hear them.

Gradually the shouts came further and further apart. No more people tramped across the bridge. Quiet settled down. Adam could not tell whether any of the de Veseys had been caught or not; he fervently hoped not. He wondered what had happened to the dog.

If only Nick were there to snuggle close and keep him from feeling so alone and frightened!

His harp was gone too. Andrew still had it. What was the proverb that Roger used to quote? "A loan seldom comes laughing home." A fine time it was to remember that!

News of Roger

Long before morning Adam decided that he
would not go on with the de Veseys, even
if he could find them again. They were the
wrong kind of minstrels. He did not want to
be like them any more than he wanted to be
a parish clerk; he was going to be a real minstrel like Roger. He had lost his harp, it was
true, but twice before this he had thought it
was gone and had got it back again; perhaps
this time too he would recover it. What he
must do, he told himself, breathing on his stiff
fingers to warm them, was to go straight
back to London and de Lisle House.

For a little while he thought of stopping to

see Jill and John Ferryman, but he decided against that. They would be kind and welcoming, but he had no time to spare. Our Lady's Day was already past and December almost half gone.

Afraid to venture out from his hiding place till it was light, and afraid to go to sleep there, he recited the tale of Havelok the Dane to himself to keep awake. He knew it best of all Roger's tales, probably because he liked it best. When he was a real minstrel, and he was going to start being one tomorrow, this was the tale he would tell oftenest, and now was as good a time to practice as any other.

"Soon after the king of Denmark was laid in his grave," he whispered, "the Earl Godard took the young prince Havelok and his sisters and shut them away in a tower, where they had nothing but the long mutter of the sea to keep them company. They were too young, poor children, to understand that the earl was seizing all their land and forcing their people to swear obedience to him, but they knew that they were hungry and cold."

Saying the words over to himself in the dark and cold under the bridge, Adam thought that he had never really understood Havelok before. In spite of yesterday's mutton and meat pie he was hungry again and so cold that he ached all over. Pretending that the icy stream slipping past in the blackness was a roomful of people, he went on with the tale: how the evil Godard hired Grim the fisherman to carry Havelok out in a sack and drown him, how at midnight a golden light shimmered all around the sack and stood up from Havelok's mouth like a flower stem, and how Grim knew from that he was the true lord of Denmark.

" 'Lord, forgive me,' cried Grim, kneeling at Havelok's feet. 'I will take care of you till you can ride a horse and bear spear and helmet, and Godard shall not know you are alive. I'll bring you milk and bread and cheese and custard pastries — fine fare if I do say so. It's true enough, the old proverb, "Whom God will help, no man can harm." '

"When Havelok had eaten his fill, Grim made a soft bed for him, undressed him and put him in it, saying, 'Sleep, son, sleep tight, and fear nothing. Your sorrow has turned to joy.'

"Milk and bread and cheese and custard pastries," repeated hungry Adam, but when the first gray streaks of morning light came, he said stoutly, "whom God will help, no man can harm," and, scrambling out from under the bridge, he washed his face in the river, and set forth.

He took the path along the river, but turned to the left before he came to the ferry and made his way over a hill and down again into a thick beech wood. The morning mist curled up among the wet, dark gray trunks of the trees. Once he met a fox with a chicken in his mouth and once a squirrel scolded him shrilly from a bough overhead, but except for them he seemed to be alone in an empty world.

The path climbed another hill and this time brought him out on an open height covered with fine grass which was green still in spite of the cold. The sun was up now and glistened on the wet stones of a little chapel which had been built there for the spiritual comfort of pilgrims. It looked lonely and forlorn now, for few pilgrims came this way in winter. Beyond the valley, where mist rose from a river hidden among the trees, the bare downs hunched their shoulders into the sunshine and the broken chalk tracks of the Way gleamed white and dazzling.

In the valley were villages, Shere and Gomshall and Wotton, but Adam took the path up over the downs. He did not want to meet people who might question him, and particularly he did not want to go to Gomshall. Its name had risen so readily to Lawrence's tongue last night that Adam thought it must be a place the de Veseys were in the habit of going to. He felt kindly toward Jack and Alison (especially Alison) and Andrew and Lawrence, but he did not wish to meet them today, not even to get his harp back.

As he walked along in the cold sunshine he thought about all the things he had lost and presently he found himself making up a song about them.

"Silver pennies once I had," he sang to a little tune that seemed to come with the words,

> "Jingling pennies made me glad,
>   Now they're gone from me.
> Where they are I do not know,
> Like an arrow from a bow
>   They are gone from me."

It was a nuisance not having his harp, but his hands were so swollen and sore with chilblains that he could not have played it very well anyhow. He was lucky not to have a sore throat. He made the next verse about the harp.

"Once a harp hung by my side,
  Merry music was my guide,
    Now it's gone from me.
  Where it is I cannot tell,
  Like the leaves that slowly fell
    It is gone from me."

He felt dreadfully sad when he sang about his harp. It wasn't as if Andrew could really play it; all he could do was pick out a few chords. Losing his harp was the next thing to losing Nick.

"Once I had a little dog,
  Gaily down the road we'd jog,
    Now he's gone from me.
  Where he is I cannot say
  Like the winds of yesterday
    He is gone from me."

Now the sun went under a cloud, and everything at once looked grayer and bleaker and colder.

"Sorrow to my heart is come," Adam sang. Losing Roger was the worst, but somehow it made him feel a little better to find words and a tune for it. "Cold has made my fingers numb." Actually, instead of being numb, they were hurting fiercely, but *numb* rhymed.

At this point he came on a peddler who was sitting on his pack and eating his dinner by the side of the path. Good, he thought. If he was really going to be a minstrel, here was his chance to begin.

Now more than ever Adam wished for his harp; he scarcely knew how to announce himself without it. He was painfully aware that he did not look like a minstrel in his brown cloak and hood.

Suddenly he threw himself on his hands and turned cartwheels in a circle all around the astonished peddler, who stopped chewing and let his mouth hang open while he watched.

"Good morrow, fair sir," said Adam, when he was right side up again. He found that he was a little breathless, but not dizzy. Good. "Wouldn't you like a little minstrelsy with your dinner? It cheers the heart and aids digestion. All the great lords know that, or why would they give minstrels gifts of fine coats and dapple-gray war horses?"

"I have no coats nor war horses to give away," said the peddler morosely. "If I had, I'd be wearing one and riding the other, and I wouldn't be here, I'd be in Naples where it's warm." He took a bite out of the chicken leg he held in his hand. More of the chicken lay on a bit of linen cloth on the ground beside him. Adam eyed it hungrily.

"I'll tell you the tale of Havelok the Dane for a penny," he said persuasively, "or I'll sing you a song that no one has ever heard before for the drumstick."

The peddler looked up at Adam with a sudden softening in his wrinkled, monkeylike little face. "Hungry?" he said.

Adam nodded.

"Drumstick first," said the peddler. "Song afterward."

It was the best drumstick that Adam had ever tasted, roasted to a turn and well flavored and full of meat. He ate every scrap and then he sucked the bone. How he wished he could give that bone to Nick!

The peddler watched him. "Have a wing," he suggested.

"Song next," said Adam, licking his fingers.

Holding his arm as if he had a harp and plucking the air where the strings should be, he sang the song he had just made that morning; and as he sang, the rest of the last stanza came to him.

"Sorrow to my heart is come,
   Cold has made my fingers numb,
      Hunger has its sting.
Still I'll sing through every day
Till my sadness goes away
      Like winter in the spring."

"Winter!" exclaimed the peddler. "How I hate it. A nasty, cold, wet, disagreeable season."

He did not say whether he liked the song or not, but he held out a piece of the breast instead of a wing and Adam decided that he would rather have food than praise.

"Live around here?" asked the peddler.

"I'm a minstrel," replied Adam proudly. "I live on the road."

"You don't look like much of a minstrel, but you can sing, all right. Spend last night in Guildford?"

"Not right *in* Guildford," replied Adam cautiously. "Near it. Why?"

"Which way'd you come?" persisted the peddler.

"Over the hill with the chapel," said Adam.

"St. Martha's. You must have been down at Shalford. Did the hue and cry spread down there?"

"I don't know," said Adam, quaking inside. "Did — " his voice wavered but he forced himself to go on as carelessly as he could, "did they raise the hue and cry in Guildford?"

"*Did* they? I was there and I was out shouting with the rest of them. A band of robbers came in after curfew and the watch found them trying to break into that new Flemish glover's shop. Ten of them there were, great giants of men! They knocked down the watch and stamped on him."

"Did they get caught?" asked Adam anxiously.

"Caught! Can you catch a mad bull? All Guildford was out after them, but nobody could hold them. One of them went past me with his eyes gleaming red in the dark like the king of Hell himself."

It was all Adam could do not to laugh outright at this picture of five thin, frightened minstrels. Roger used to say that the faster news ran the bigger it grew.

"Where are they now?" he asked.

The peddler raised his hands and let them drop. "Gone," he said dramatically. "Clean gone. Probably they have a hideout somewhere."

Adam wondered what the peddler would

do if he were to say suddenly: "One of them is sitting beside you this minute. Boo!" Reluctantly he gave up the idea, though it would be fun. At any rate, the de Veseys had escaped. Now Adam need think about them no more.

He told the peddler all about his adventure with Daun William and Sir Robert de Rideware; and the peddler, who had known the merchant somewhere, was so interested that he gave Adam half a penny. The silver penny with King Edward's head on it was the only coin minted in England then, but people sometimes broke them in two and used the halves.

They went on together till they came almost to Burford Bridge, and then the peddler turned south to Dorking and Adam went on to the inn in Westhumble Lane where he and Roger had slept that night nearly four months ago, the night that Nick had been stolen.

The innkeeper and his energetic wife and the old gaffer all came running when the maid first saw Adam and called out that he was back.

"Wherever have you been?" demanded Dame Clarice. "And your poor father hunting for you high and low all over the south of England!"

"I've been in Winchester," answered Adam, feeling that her tone of blame was undeserved, but not taking the time to explain. "Do you know where Roger is?"

"In Winchester? It's very strange that he didn't see you there. He looked for you all over the city and all over the Fair, and he could have got your dog for you if you had been there, but the magistrate could not seem to get the story straight in his mind without seeing you."

"Where's Roger now?" insisted Adam, ready to jump out of his skin with suspense.

"Where's your harp?" put in the gaffer. "You used to make good music with that harp."

"I lent it to a fellow who didn't give it back," said Adam. "Is Roger in London?"

"That was careless of you." said Clarice disapprovingly. "What will Roger say to that?"

"Don't torture the lad," protested the innkeeper. "Let me tell him where his father is. He's gone to London to the de Lisles, boy. He thought perhaps you had remembered that he had to be back for Christmas and had gone looking for him there. He came here from Winchester to get the horse, and then he rode back to Winchester again hunting for you. Now and then he met somebody who told him a lad had been looking for a minstrel and a dog, but he never did find you. So he went off to London, thinking you must be there."

Adam's spirits soared. Roger had not disappeared from the face of the earth. Roger had not forgotten all about him. (He felt ashamed that in his most unhappy moments he had almost thought that.) Roger was riding all over southern England on Bayard looking for him, and tomorrow he would go straight to London and find Roger. Then together they would find Jankin and get Nick back.

"What Have You Done with Him?"

Two days later Adam crossed London Bridge in a thick fog which so hid and changed familiar landmarks that he wondered if he would be able to find his way to de Lisle House. It was chilly and wet and rather suffocating, and the people whom he met were beaded all over with tiny drops of moisture and had a straining look in their eyes.

It was not the way he had imagined coming back to London, but perhaps it was even better. As he made his groping way through the muffled city and out again at Ludgate, he imagined afresh the end of his long road. He saw himself entering the hall at de Lisle House, where a fire would be burning brightly. He saw Roger coming toward him, his gray eyes under the broad brow shining with joy, and at Roger's heels, ears flopping, silky sides gleaming in the firelight, would be Nick. Then Roger would hug Adam till he lifted him clean off the floor, and that night he would say as Grim had said to Havelok, "Sleep, son, sleep tight, and fear nothing. Your sorrow has turned to joy."

The road beyond Temple Bar was so deep in mud that Adam went squelching in almost to his knees at every step. Dark lurked beyond the whiteness of the fog; now and then a ghostly building loomed up and vanished. Adam was so tired after his long day's march that only the thought of what he would find when he got there kept him wearily plodding on till he came to the de Lisle gatehouse.

He knocked at the wooden door, and after endless minutes the porter came to open it.

"Oh, it's you," he said. "Come in. But they're all away."

"Away?" repeated Adam, unable to believe his ears.

"That's what I said. Come in."

"Roger too?"

"And why not? His place is with his lord at Christmastime."

Adam kicked at a cobblestone with his squelching shoes and fought to steady his quivering mouth, to keep the tears that stung behind his eyes from spilling over. His heart felt as if it would burst. The porter put a kindly hand on his shoulder and led him across the courtyard to the hall door.

"He looked everywhere for you before he went," he said, "and he left messages for you too. He said you could stay here till someone should be going to Ludlow and then go along with whoever it is. He'll pick you up there in May."

May! But that was months away! Adam sniffed loudly and wiped his nose with the tail of his wet cloak.

"Where is he now?" he asked.

"He's with Sir Edmund, who's with the lord king putting down the rebellion in Wales."

"Wales!" repeated Adam forlornly. It sounded as far away as the moon, or Scotland.

"The rest of the de Lisles are at Ludlow, but I'm here and the bailiff and his family are here. So pull yourself together and make the best of it."

De Lisle House in the winter, with only a few people rattling around in it like a handful of dried peas in a bushel basket, was altogether a different place from de Lisle House in the summer, when Sir Edmund and Lady Richenda sat at the high table and Simon carved for them, when Margery and Hugh and the rest played London Bridge in the garden and Emilie made ready for her wedding, when Roger and the other minstrels sang and told tales. Now it was dim and empty and drafty. The fine glass in the windows was gone, and fog seeped in around the edges of the heavy wooden shutters. The tapestries had been taken from the walls, the silver dishes and candlesticks from the open cupboard shelves, and the bright silk cushions from chairs and benches. A fire burned on the hearth in the center, but even with the vent open above, the smoke hung low in a cloud instead of rising.

Adam had a good supper that night and afterward an audience for the story of his adventures. He had a hot bath and a warm bed to sleep in, and a maid servant took away his clothes to dry and brush them for him.

He would not have to hide under a bridge again or tramp long miles when he was tired and cold. Still he lay awake late into the night, longing for Roger, longing for Nick, wondering how he was to fill the flat and empty months ahead. It would be better when he got to Ludlow where Hugh and Margery were, but who would be going to Ludlow in the winter? And suppose Roger should be hurt, or killed? They were fighting in Wales, weren't they?

In the morning, Matthew the bailiff's son came to bring Adam his clothes and waken him.

"I'm glad you've come back," said Matthew sitting down on the edge of the bed. "It's been lonely since Hugh and Godfrey and the others went to Ludlow. My cousin Agnes — you saw her last night — has come from Uxbridge to spend the winter and be trained by my mother. She's dreadful," he finished flatly.

Adam had not cared so much for Matthew as for the other members of Hugh's company, but now they were drawn together by their common feeling about Agnes.

She was a busy, bossy, self-satisfied young thing, tossing her long yellow hair proudly and walking with her stomach out. She had light blue eyes, slightly popped, and a full red mouth which she kept pursed up in a disapproving way. She called Adam "Boy" and ordered him to bring her stool or the book off the shelf or to fetch her a comfit from the cupboard, as if she were the lady of the house. Her name meant lamb of God, she said, but to Adam she was just a silly sheep, and not a sheep of God either. He occupied dull moments with thinking up humiliating accidents for her to fall into, which he would see, turning aside to hide his smile; but he contented himself meanwhile with answering her lofty remarks with a derisive "Baa."

It was no way for a minstrel to behave, he realized that, but then at de Lisle House they did not treat him as a minstrel; to them he was a rather tiresome boy who had been left in the bailiff's care.

As often as they could, he and Matthew escaped from the house and from Agnes and went sightseeing, sometimes in London and sometimes in Westminster.

Christmas came soon and lasted twelve days, from the Feast of the Nativity till Twelfth Night. Nothing much went on at de Lisle House with just the bailiff's family

there. The Yule log was brought into the hall with a rather feeble fanfare and kindled from the remains of the Yule log of the year before. The bailiff's wife handed out some battered masks, and they capered about in dragons' heads and asses' heads and tried to pretend they were very merry. Adam sang some carols, but as he hadn't his harp and as *his voice* would *quaver unhappily, they were not very convincing.*

He kept remembering last Christmas which he and Roger and Nick spent at a manor house in Yorkshire. That had been a real Christmas, with joy and minstrelsy. All the young people in the hall had danced and sung the holly and the ivy carol, with the boys bringing in the holly from one side and the girls carrying in the ivy from the other. After they had danced, singing round in circles, the holly chased the ivy around the hall till everybody was breathless with laughing. This year nobody laughed as if he meant it.

On New Year's Eve the wassailers came with a big bowl of hot spiced ale in which roasted apples were floating, and everybody had a drink of it.

"Wassail!" the cry rang out under the high oak ceiling in the hall, and "Drink

Hail!" the answer came ringing out.

The bailiff gave the wassailers some money and they went off singing a carol.

The people at de Lisle House the next day exchanged New Year's gifts. Adam had told the tale of Havelok at Gracechurch Market and got enough pennies to buy walnuts for Matthew and some figs for the porter, but nobody remembered to give him anything The chief feature of the day was the way Agnes went about with a Cheshire cat grin on her face, announcing that she got more gifts than anyone else.

Away from de Lisle House there were plenty of festivities that really were gay, and Adam and Matthew went to as many of them as they could manage to wriggle and squeeze their way into. They went to the Christmas play at St. Clement's and saw the shepherds give the Christ Child gifts of a ball and a bird and a bob of cherries. On the Eve of the Feast of the Innocents they were in the crowd that gathered at St. Paul's to watch the Boy Bishop.

A lad of their own age, all dressed up like a bishop with mitre and robes, walked at the head of a procession of boys into the cathedral and performed the whole service. He even preached a sermon in Latin.

"Do you suppose he made that up himself?" said Matthew skeptically.

"I bet I could," said Adam, wagging his head. "I wish I was him. I bet I could have done it better." This Boy Bishop was handsome but stiff. A boy with minstrel's training, like himself, could have done it, Adam thought, with an air.

A man standing next to him had heard what he said. "Do you know how to make music on a trumpet?" the man asked abruptly.

Adam's hands ached for his lost harp. "I play a harp," he said, "and Roger was going to teach me to play the viol. Anybody can play a trumpet that can draw in a big breath and blow."

"What I was leading to was this," said the man pointedly: "He who blows well puts the narrow end to his mouth and the wide end outward."

Adam scuffled his feet uneasily. The man meant that he had been boasting. Roger used to say that he had a tendency that way. It took him a little while to recover from this uncomfortable episode.

As the king was keeping Christmas court

in Conway Castle in Wales this year, Westminster was quiet, but still one holiday
tournament was held, and Adam and Matthew went to watch. The crowd was so thick
that all they really saw was the coming and
going of knights and ladies and heralds, and
the crowds of minstrels and tumblers and
jugglers. They heard the trumpets and the
shouting, the whinnying of horses and the
stamp of their feet, the clash of lances and
shields. Adam had never in all his life seen
so many shields of arms blazoned in bright
colors with lions and wyvers, with chevrons
and fountains and sheaves. He thought of
Perkin and wished — as he so often did —
that he were here instead of the well-mean
ing but dull boy beside him.

In the streets of London every night during
the Christmas season great bonfires blazed
high in the sky to clear the air and to give
cheer. Wealthy citizens put bread and drink
on tables before their doors, and anybody
who was hungry might help himself, as long
as the supply lasted. In the daytime bands
of apprentices had wrestling matches and
archery contests in the open fields. Oh, there
was plenty to see and to enjoy away from
de Lisle House.

After Twelfth Night came Plow Monday, when everybody went back to work. In the country beyond St. Clement Danes, the villeins began to plow the fields for the planting of the lenten seed: oats, peas, beans, barley, and the vetches.

The cold and gloomy days crept on, with dark coming after evensong and the long evenings full of Agnes and the sort of baby games she liked. Then came a stretch of bitter weather, so cold that the Fleet Stream froze over, and Londoners went sliding on the ice with the shinbones of animals strapped to the soles of their feet. They used poles tipped with iron to push themselves along, and they could work up a speed that was almost — so they shouted happily to one another — like flying.

The older ones propelled themselves with solemn joy, in straight lines, but the younger fry played tag, or jousted, using their poles as lances. There was many a tumble and not a few battered heads and bruised arms, but no one was badly hurt.

Adam, having begged a couple of shinbones from one of the foreign butchers in Butcher's Row on the Strand, stayed out all day as long as the ice lasted. The cold, clear air, the swift motion, and the joy of friendships made on the moment kept him from churning over and over in his mind his discontent at de Lisle House and the longing for Roger that gnawed at him without stopping.

One afternoon when the bells of St. Clement's were calling out "oranges and lemons" faintly over the frozen fields, Adam, careless for a moment of where he was going, bumped head-on into a man coming from the other direction. The impact made them both gasp, but only Adam, who was the lighter, took a tumble. The man reached out a hand to help him up, and Adam, as he scrambled to his feet, saw the gay-colored short surcoat of a minstrel. The next moment he was looking straight into Jankin's face.

With a yell Adam flung himself on Jankin, and down they both went in a tangle of poles and shinbones and legs, with Adam on the whole on top.

"Where's Nick?" he shouted, sitting astride Jankin and bouncing on his stomach for emphasis. "What have you done with him?"

Everybody in the vicinity came rushing up to see what was happening. A man seized Adam by the shoulders and tried to pull him off.

"Let me alone!" he roared. "He stole my dog! Where is he? Where is Nick?"

Jankin groaned. "Get off me," he said, "and I'll tell you."

Reluctantly Adam freed Jankin, but stood and glowered down at him, ready to pounce again if he should try to run away.

Jankin sat up and felt himself all over tenderly; his face cleared. "Nothing broken, no thanks to you," he said. "I haven't got your dog, boy, and that's the truth. He chewed his leash one night near Gorhambury and the next morning he was gone. I searched everywhere but I couldn't find him. I was sorry I took him, after I heard at the ferry under St. Catherine's Hill on the way back from the Fair how you'd swum the river for him. I didn't know you set so much store by him. I didn't want the horse — cost too much to feed — so I took the dog instead. If you ever find him, you can have dog and horse both."

Adam's eyes searched Jankin's thin, dark, vivid face. Could he believe him? Jankin returned his look squarely. "It was near Gorhambury I lost him," he said, "about two weeks ago."

The crowd, losing interest, began to slide off. Jankin clapped Adam on the back. "Have good day," he said cheerfully. "I hope you, find him. He was a good little dog, though he never cared much for me." He picked up his pole and pushed himself off.

Still Adam stood there, rumpled from his tussle, his hood pushed back on his shoulders, his cap on the ice at his feet, and his tousled sandy head bare in the wind. "Gorhambury," he was thinking. "It's near St. Alban's. Nick's gone back to Dame Malkin's looking for me. There's where Nick is!"

Adam's Song

"Iron lying still soon gathers rust,
A stagnant pool is slimy,
The harp unplucked is thick with rust,
Most things not used grow grimy.

"The highway is the minstrel's home,
   He's working when he's playing;
   He's never lost if far he roam —
   He wanders when he's staying.

"I've gathered rust and dust too long,
   I need the wind and rain!
   I'll tell my tale and sing my song
   Out on the road again!"

A DAM sang aloud as he stepped out on the
     road leading west from St. Alban's.
Hoarfrost silvered every twig and holly leaf
in the thicket beside the road, and when the
sun suddenly came out the whole world shone
and glittered like the fairy country in the
"Lay of Sir Orfeo." In the frozen ruts thin
layers of white ice broke under his feet with
a tinkling sound. Overhead great companies
of rooks careered about in the sky cawing and
calling.

It was nearly a week since Adam had left
de Lisle House. The bailiff and his wife had
let him go without protest; it was easy to

see that they had not been overpleased to be saddled with the care of the minstrel's son. The porter, on the other hand, had given him a penny and a packet of food, and some careful directions about finding Roger.

"Stay at St. Alban's school," he said, "or go on to Ludlow, or come back here. Don't do any more seesawing back and forth from village to village, and try to land on your feet instead of your head."

Agnes, curiously enough, had been much annoyed at his departure. She had scowled and pouted and said crossly that she didn't see why he cared so much about a dog. Matthew had walked part way with him the first day and seemed depressed when he said good-bye.

"I don't suppose you'll come back," he said, "even after you get Nick."

"I don't suppose I will," Adam had answered.

He liked Matthew, but he did not want to go back to de Lisle House without Roger. Idling about the great, empty house when the de Lisles were away was no life for a minstrel. His place was on the road.

He had spent three days at St. Alban's

with Dame Malkin, and now he was on his way to Oxford, whither Perkin had gone — with Nick.

"Yes, Nick was here," the dame had said, sitting hunched on a stool beside her fire and beaming up at Adam with deep-wrinkled, frosty blue eyes, "I heard a scratching at the door outside and a whining, and when I went to open it, there he was with a broken leash trailing. He was thin as a twig and his ears were all full of mud and burrs, but by my faith, he was happy. He jumped all over me, crying out for joy, and then he ran sniffing all over the house looking for you."

"Where is he now?" Adam cried.

The dame had looked miserable. "I couldn't keep him. It's wintertime, and there is so little food. I gave him my dinner that day — and how his sides bulged out after he ate it! So Perkin took him with him. He was off to Oxford, begging his way. He said he could as well beg for two as one. He's keeping him for you. He said you'd come to Oxford to see him."

Adam stayed three days at St. Alban's because Dame Malkin could not bear to let him go. He got his meals at the abbey guesthouse, but he slept in the cottage beside the fire and in the long evenings he told his old friend of his adventures. "It's better than any minstrel's romance," she would sigh. "Eh, lad, no wonder you're taller and have a thinner line to your chin."

The masters at St. Alban's school welcomed him more affectionately than he had ever imagined they would, and once again he sang the Latin hymns with the choir at evensong. He marveled, as he looked at the school boys, how young they were, and he remembered with amazement that less than a year ago he himself had been as young as that.

Now he was off for Oxford to find Perkin and get Nick again. Among all the scholars at the University surely there would be some who liked minstrelsy and were not too poor to pay for it. He would stay there till spring, and then he would go on to Ludlow to meet Roger.

His heart was filled with a deep content to be out on the road once more. He sang over the song that he had made about it. A road — how clearly he remembered Roger's saying it — was a kind of sacred place.

If only he had his harp, he thought, and if only his shoes were not so worn. Dame Malkin had exclaimed over them. "You'll never get to Oxford on those soles!" she cried.

"Country people wear wooden clogs to save their shoes. Couldn't you do that? I've an old pair you can have."

"I couldn't walk miles in wooden clogs," objected Adam. "They'd break my feet. These will last — they've got to."

She had given him some rags to pad them with, but they were still uncomfortably thin on the hard, frozen ruts, and chilly too. Now that his attention had been called to them, he kept examining them anxiously at intervals to see if the holes got any larger. He thought they did.

Never having been to Oxford, he did not know just how to get there. Dame Malkin told him to be sure to go to Ewelme, for Perkin's father lived there and no doubt he would help Adam on his way. She showed him the road to Watford, which was sure to be the first stage of the journey.

He came to Watford by noon, and offered to tell the tale of King Horn at the inn in return for his dinner. Unfortunately his memory failed him and he got stuck in the middle of it. The words that Roger used to say would not come, and worse still he could not remember what happened well enough to tell it in his own words. Somebody laughed as he stood red-faced and shamed, and several others, ignoring Adam altogether, began to talk about the weather.

It was Candlemas Day, February second, and the sun was shining.

"If Candlemas Day be fair and bright
   Winter will have another flight,"

quoted a burly-looking man in a thick fur-lined mantle,

"But if it be dark with clouds and rain
   Winter is gone and will not come again."

He himself looked as if he were well fed and warmly dressed enough not to care if winter stayed forever, but everyone else was pinched and thin and pale.

Adam knew better than to try to regain attention by competing with the conversation; he contributed to it instead.

"Si sol splendescat Maria purificante," he recited the Latin version of the old saw, "major erit glacies post festum quam fuit ante."

The Latin startled the room into momentary silence, and Adam seized his chance.

"I can sing, lordings," he said.

Without waiting for permission he sang the song he had made, and after that, "Winter wakens all my care." They liked the second one better. Then he told them news of St. Alban's, how the hares and rabbits had eaten the bark off an apple tree in Master John's garden all the way round the trunk as high up as they could reach and the tree would die surely; how Harry the miller had not got his oats in yet but his old ewe had had twin lambs three weeks ago; how the first pair of partridges had been seen in the wood near St. Stephen's Church the day that Adam got there.

"Oh, spring is on the way," said the burly man, "though it comes slowly. Here, Sir Innkeeper, give this boy his dinner and I will pay."

When Adam was ready to go, the innkeeper told him to follow the river Coln to Rickmansworth, and gave him a message to take to his brother the smith there.

"Tell him the baby is a girl," he said. "We're naming her Cecilia. The christening will be after matins next Sunday and tell him to be sure to come."

Adam spent that night with the blacksmith of Rickmansworth, who was immensely pleased with the news about the baby. "That's the first girl born in our family in ninety-nine years," he said.

The smith was a man of substance in Rickmansworth. He was a freeholder and paid rent for his smithy and his holding of four acres instead of doing work for the lord of the manor. Besides the money payment he had to give the lord a hundred horseshoes a year, fifty with nails and fifty without, and he had to shoe the steward's hackney whenever it needed it at a penny for four shoes, but that was far better than having to drop his own work just when he was busiest and go plowing or reaping for the lord.

He was busy now sharpening plowshares and coulters for the spring plowing, and Adam perched on the windowsill and shouted to him above the din of the anvil as he worked.

"I wish I could get two shoes for a half-penny," shrilled Adam.

"Would you like them nailed on?" roared back the smith, and Adam had to admit that he would not.

That night it snowed. The next morning the smith's eldest son put Adam on the way to Amersham. The snow had drifted thick on the road, but on the fields it lay thin, giving them a dappled effect, white where the little hollows were filled, and purply brown where the humps were bare. It was easier to walk on the fields than in the road, but even so before the day was half gone Adam's big toe had come through his right shoe.

When he came to a river and stopped to get a drink, he saw where little creatures had been before him: Rabbit footprints were there with the forefeet together and the hind feet in line, like a Y, and there were too the deep, pointed tracks of birds, partridges, he supposed, and smaller tracks that might be thrushes.

There was no sun today and the wind was sharp. He was glad when he came into a beech wood, where the trees, bright green with moss, broke the wind but let light through. Under bushes where the snow had not penetrated, the fallen leaves still kept their deep gold color, so that the wood not only felt warmer than the open fields, but looked warmer too.

From Amersham Adam pushed on over the hills to Chipping Wycombe, which he was lucky enough to strike on a market day. He was tired out when he got there, and his big toe had come through his left shoe, but he found a welcome in the house of an apothecary who was in high good humor because he had had a successful day.

The next day it rained, and the next; the third day was gray and heavy, with dark clouds lumbering across the sky, covering swiftly any patches of watery blue that might show for a little while. The road was so deep in mud, and so steep, and so slippery that Adam could not get any farther than Fingest that day. He was as tired at the end of it as if he had tramped a dozen miles instead of six and a half. A cotter let him sleep in his hay barn, which was warm and fragrant. In the morning Adam put hay in his shoes to cover up the holes, but it did not make them any more comfortable.

From Fingest to Watlington the road went past the Bishop of Lincoln's palace, and climbed high up over the ridge of the Chilterns, where it crossed the ancient Roman Icknield Way, and plunged steeply down again on the other side. It went through thick woods and sometimes all but disappeared in a tangle of bushes and saplings. Scarcely anyone was out that day, and Adam felt lonely and sometimes even a little frightened as he struggled up the steep places, over rocks, and around muddy pools that seemed to have no bottom.

In that inn at Watlington was the steward of the Abbey of Bec, who spent his life, poor man, traveling from one manor to another of the abbey's vast possessions, holding court and settling suits. In the last two weeks, he said wearily, he had covered a hundred and fifty miles and held courts in a dozen different manors. He had several men with him, and they all looked at Adam in surprise when he stepped forward in his shabby brown mantle, with his muddy toes sticking out of his shoes, and offered to entertain them with tales of love and adventure.

At first the steward, who was an important man as well as a tired one and had troublesome problems on his mind, waved Adam away impatiently, but then he called him back and told him he might try.

Adam considered telling the tale of Havelok, which he was sure he would not forget, but decided that the steward, who spoke French with a French accent, would not care for such a very English story. He was afraid to attempt the "Lay of Sir Orfeo" without his harp, and so he sang songs instead. Something made him choose first a lullaby that his mother used to sing to him years ago:

> "Lullay, mine liking, my dear son,
>   my sweeting,
>   Lullay, dear heart, my own son, my
>   darling."

Afterward, because the steward was connected with an abbey, he sang the Latin hymn "Stabat Mater."

This was wise, for the steward's head ached with weariness, and Adam's voice, so fresh and clear and soaring, carried him away far beyond the untidy little inn and the thought of tomorrow's traveling.

When Adam stopped, the room was silent. Then the steward thanked him gravely and asked him why he was alone and where he was going. After Adam told his story, the abbot's steward said: "If when you get to Oxford, my son, you should decide that you would like to stay there and study, go to see my friend the Warden of Merton College. Tell him I sent you and that I think he could be of help to you and you perhaps to him."

He gave Adam five pennies, and Adam had supper and a share of a bed that night, and three pennies left over.

He spent the next morning trying to buy a pair of shoes in Watlington for three pence.

He thought perhaps someone might have a pair that was worn but still sound which he did not need, but the only shoes he could find were so big that he walked out of them at the first step. So he had to set out for Ewelme in shoes with no soles at all.

Soon the worn uppers flapped so irritatingly that he took them off and went on in his torn hose. When these too wore through, he limped on over the cold wet ruts in his bare feet.

By midafternoon the winter day began to draw in. Between the high, windswept fields the road stretched muddy and rutted toward bare purple woods. Here and there a swollen brook flooding the road reflected the cold cherry-colored light of the setting sun. Shadows came out of the hedges as if driven out by the rising wind. Adam felt small and lost as he trudged along under the enormous sky. He thought of the little creatures that shared this edge of the world with him, the mice, the rabbits, the partridges, and felt sorry for them in the wind and cold. At last a valley opened before him; he saw a thin twist of blue smoke rising over the tops of trees, and heard, faint on the wind, the sound of church bells.

Adam Helps a Plowman

ADAM came down the hill into Ewelme just as the villagers filed into the square-towered little stone church for evensong, and followed the last one in. It would be no use to go looking for the plowman's house if everyone was at service.

The little church was cold and dim, with only the wax candles on the altar to light it, and the stone floor was even colder to Adam's feet than the road had been. He stood at the back of the congregation of villagers uncomfortably shifting his weight from one aching foot to the other.

Suddenly he felt a little movement among

the people, and then a nudge at his elbow. He turned, and all but cried out with joy in the middle of the prayer. Perkin!

He looked the same as ever, slender and dark and erect, with clear brown eyes and a serious smile. The astonishing thing was that Adam no longer looked up into Perkin's face; it was now on the level with his own. For the first time he realized how he had grown during these past months.

He squeezed Perkin's arm as he used to do in school at St. Alban's, and Perkin squeezed his back. When they knelt for the blessing, Perkin leaned over to whisper in his ear: "I've got Nick for you."

They were the first out of the church when evensong was over. Lickety split they went across the churchyard and over the low wall in a shortcut to Perkin's house.

"Nick!" called Adam. "Nick! I'm coming!"

Answering came a shrill yelp of joy.

The next moment dog and boy were together again. Adam tried to hug the warm silky body close to him, while Nick wriggled and darted and jumped, now licking Adam's face thoroughly, now planting big feathery paws on Adam's chest, now twisting till his red tongue flopped beside his rapturous tail first on one side and then on the other. When

Adam unfastened the rope by which he was tied, Nick raced in circles all over the yard, yelping with joy, while the cat jumped spitting up a tree, the chickens ran squawking in all directions, the geese stretched out their necks and hissed, and Adam and Perkin sat back on their heels and yelled with laughter.

In the midst of all this joy, Perkin's family joined them: his father Wat, the plowman, his mother Gunnilda, his elder brother Robin, and his younger brother Dickon.

That evening they had one of Gunnilda's famous kidney pies for supper, and sat late around the fire to talk, Adam's bare feet on Nick and his arm around Perkin's neck, their heads leaning against each other in the old way, the sleek black head and the tousled sandy one. Adam thought he had never met a family he liked so well as Perkin's: Wat, slow of speech, gentle, and big; Gunnilda, thin and dark like Perkin, with warm, intelligent eyes like his; Robin, tall and awkward and kind; and Dickon, little and eager, with bright shy eyes like a field mouse.

When they went to bed in the room above, Adam and Perkin lay awake whispering for a long time.

"I thought you'd be in Oxford," Adam said in Perkin's ear.

"I would have been, but I came home first, and Father needed help with the plowing. He's the lord's plowman now, and he gets paid for it, but it doesn't leave him time to plant his own strips unless he has help. Robin is his oxherd, and he is a good one, but Dickon is too little to be much use."

"I'll help," said Adam promptly.

"You'll have to stay anyhow till you get some shoes and things," said Perkin. "No one would think you were a minstrel now. You look more like a beggar."

He poked Adam in the ribs as he said that, to show that he was making a joke, and Nick at the foot of the bed woke up and came walking up Adam's body to lick both their faces till they burrowed in the bedstraw to keep him off and muffle their giggles. But all the same Adam was troubled. A true joke is no joke, as the proverb said — and how was he to get new shoes and a minstrel's surcoat?

"If you'd stay till the planting's done and take my place here," said Perkin, "I could go on to Oxford. Mother would help you with your things. Lent begins next week anyhow, and there won't be much chance for minstrelsy then."

So it was arranged. A few days later Perkin, with his precious book under one arm, his bundle of clothes on his back, and a basket of bread and cheese and onions on the other arm, started out to walk the fourteen miles to Oxford and a learned career. Adam, the minstrel's son, with clogs on his bare feet, began to be a farmer's boy.

Wat had a team of four oxen, small thin beasts, but strong and willing.

"They're almost human," Robin said, his eyes warm with love for them, "as human as a dog any day."

He slept in the stable with them at night, on a bed of hay where he could hear their breathing and speak to them lovingly from time to time. All good oxherds slept with their oxen, he told Adam.

"I like horses better," said Adam, remembering Bayard.

"Horses!" snorted Robin. "Oxen are best for plowing. A horse eats a halfpenny worth of oats every night and a shilling of grass in the summer — and there's fodder and chaff besides. An ox doesn't cost a quarter that much. A horse has to be shod too — and that's about a penny a week. Oxen have better natures too — not nearly so hasty. Give me oxen any day."

"All right, I'll give 'em to you," said Adam,

throwing a stick for Nick to run after. As for an ox being as human as a dog, that was pure nonsense.

The plow was an enormous, heavy thing made of solid oak beams, with an iron share and an iron coulter to cut and turn the sail. It took great strength to keep it straight in the furrows.

Early in the chilly mornings the four of them went out to the lord's demesne to plow the fields for barley, which was the last of the lenten seed to be planted.

Robin walked to the left of the oxen, carrying a whip and goad which he never had to use. Instead he directed them by talking to them; sometimes he even sang to them, strange tuneless chants which they seemed to understand and appreciate.

Behind the big plow walked Wat, holding the stilts or handles, and often joining in with Robin's song to the oxen. Behind Wat went Adam and Dickon with plow bats to break up the hard clods. It was strenuous work, and Adam was glad that the oxen stopped every fifty yards or so to rest for a minute or two. Even so, his shoulders ached at the end of the first few days.

In the resting time, Adam would wipe his hot face and look about him. Always there

was something to see in the winter fields. Sometimes it was a cloud of gnats dancing in the sunshine. That was a sign of spring, and away would go his mind toward Ludlow. Roger had said he would pick Adam up at Ludlow in May. When the first cuckoo called, then Adam would start out for Shropshire.

Sometimes he heard a blackbird singing or a cock-pheasant crowing. Once in the ground-ivy at the edge of the field he saw two little field mice playing. One of them climbed up the stem of a bush and nibbled at the bark.

The rabbits were breeding now, and again and again he had to call Nick back from chasing baby bunnies. Even a dog must not poach the lord's rabbits.

They plowed only till noon, and then the oxen were turned out to pasture. After dinner Wat and his family worked on their own holding. They had their garden to dig and plant with peas and beans and leeks and cabbages; they had strips of field with the other villeins for wheat and oats, rye and barley. Wat was a good farmer. He got ten bushels of wheat to the acre on the land he held. They had hens and geese to care for, several sheep, and a cow. The cow was thin, for she had spent the winter in the byre, but they were very fond of her, and the first time she was driven out to pasture with the other village cows Gunnilda was careful to tie a bit of red worsted around her tail to keep away witches.

Indoors Gunnilda worked hard too, with the cooking and the baking and cheese-making. She carded wool and washed it and dyed it and spun it; she wove it on her loom into cloth and made it into garments for her family to wear; she washed and mended their clothes too.

After evensong — Wat and his family were good church people: They paid their tithes promptly and went to service every day — they had supper, and after supper, now that Adam was with them, they had evenings of minstrelsy.

Adam sang them all the songs he knew, those he had made himself and those he had learned from Roger. He told them all the tales he could remember, and when his memory dropped out episodes here and there he invented new ones to fill the gaps. Never had he had so good an audience. The neighbors came in to listen too, and they sat scarcely blinking their eyes, and laughed or sighed with their whole hearts according to what was happening to the hero of the story. With Adam, they liked the tale of Havelok best.

"That was a fine lad," said Wat, "working the way he did as a kitchen boy — and he all the time a prince."

"Like our Adam," piped up Dickon. "He works as a plowman's boy — and he all the time a minstrel."

Everybody laughed, but Gunnilda looked startled.

The next day she took Adam aside and showed him two lengths of cloth. One she had dyed with madder a rich red, the other with woad a bright blue. "There's just enough to make you a minstrel's surcoat," she said. "I can take your old one and wash it and turn it and make it over for Dickon, and you can have the bright one."

Adam was overjoyed. March was nearly gone; the yellow blossoms were coming on the whin bushes on the common, the willows were green beside the brook, and the lord's barley was all planted. It was almost time for Adam to be going on.

While Gunnilda was cutting and fitting and stitching Adam's new surcoat, the parson who had formed a habit of dropping in to hear him sing in the evenings, brought out a piece of good leather that he had, and got the cobbler to make Adam a pair of shoes. The cobbler drew a pattern around Adam's bare feet, and then he made the shoes a little too big so that he would not soon outgrow them. They were good stout shoes, a bit clumsy, but the leather was moist and shiny and smelled new. Adam put them on the shelf until his surcoat should be finished. All he needed now was a harp.

He did not get that, but he got something else instead.

One day Wat sent him to the mill with a sack of wheat to be ground. The mill was an exciting place to go. The great wheel made a clacking and a rumbling as it turned, and the water came foaming and rushing over it. Inside it was big and dim and misty, with dark passages where candles, stuck deep in holes in the oak beams, made little pools of yellow light.

The miller put the grain Adam had brought into the hopper, from which it poured in a stream onto the great stone, and from there fell down soft and fine into the trough. When it was all ground the miller measured out the share that was his pay for grinding it, and put the rest into the sack for Adam to carry home.

"They tell me," the miller then said, jerk
ily, as if he spoke from an inner excitement
that did not show in his flour-dusted red face,
"that you're a minstrel lad with nary a harp
or a pipe to make music on."

Adam started to tell him how he had lost
his harp, but the miller was not interested.
"Come," he said mysteriously, and led the
way into his house. There from a shelf he
took down a bagpipe.

"Do you know how to play one of these?"
he asked.

Adam nodded. A shepherd in the north had
taught him three or four years ago.

"Here's the bag and these are the drones,
and this is the chanter," said the miller,
touching each one lovingly. "I never play it
anymore since I've got so heavy and my
breath is so short. You can have it," he
finished abruptly.

Adam started to say, "But I couldn't sing
to it; it takes all my breath to blow," but he
bit the words off short. He saw too plainly in
the miller's broad honest face the struggle
between the pain of sacrifice and the joy of
giving.

For an answer he filled the bag with
mighty puffs, and fumbling with the chanter,

he achieved a little tune, while the miller looked and beamed.

"Yes, that's good," he said, when Adam stopped, red-faced, to pant. "But you'll do better when you get the hang of it. It makes noble music."

Adam did not think it made noble music, though he was too polite to say so. He thought it made savage, ear-splitting noises. "I can use it to attract attention in the market-place," he said aloud, "and then when people see I'm a minstrel I can tell my tales." The idea cheered him. A bagpipe would be much better than nothing. "Oh, *thank* you!" he cried with real gratitude at last in his voice.

"People won't want any tales if they can listen to that music," said the miller happily. "Now take your flour and your pipes and get along with you, before it turns dark."

When he got back to the plowman's house, he found that Gunnilda had finished his sur-coat. She had made it of the blue cloth, with wide red sleeves, and fringed it at the hem. She had made him a round cap too, of the scraps, with red and blue pieces alternating. The dairy woman at the manor house had sent down a pair of red hose, which Gunnilda had been saving as a surprise and which she now brought out.

With a fast-beating heart, Adam put on his new clothes and new shoes, while the whole family stood around him to cheer and admire. He took the bagpipe and made Nick walk on his hind legs while he strutted and played "Sumer is i-cumen in." Then he laid down the bagpipe carefully and turned six cartwheels without stopping.

Loud Sing Cuckoo!

APRIL came. The barley pricked through the earth, spreading a yellowish green veil over the fields that Adam had helped to plow. Primroses were budding. The first swallow dipped and swooped across the sky.

Adam said good-bye regretfully to Wat and Gunnilda, Robin and Dickon and the oxen, and to all his friends in the village. They were sorry to see him go, for they had never before had a minstrel of their own, and they would miss the gaiety he brought them; but they were proud, too, that they sent him away clothed in bright clothes as a minstrel should be, with leather shoes on his feet, a bagpipe under his arm, and his dog at his heels.

Late in the afternoon he walked across the water meadows toward the walled city of Oxford. The sun was in his eyes as he came, and long shadows stretched toward him. A score of towers and spires behind the gray wall were touched with gold and purple, and on the fresh, earth-fragrant air the bells shook out silver melody.

Adam soon found that though Oxford from the outside looked like an enchanted city filled with meditative peace, inside it was so full of hurry and noise and people and confusion that it seemed as if the walls must fly apart from the pressure of it. There were almost as many church spires as there had been at Winchester, and a castle loomed up massive and threatening on its mound. There were inns and houses and shops, some fine, some mean, all jammed together, and more people on the street, Adam thought, than could ever be packed under the available roofs. Three times before he was fairly in the city he was jostled by hurrying people who seemed not even to see him. He tightened Nick's leash and walked slowly up the street, turning his head this way and that, trying to see everything at once.

He saw white friars and gray friars, he saw monks in their dark robes, students with eager faces and shabby gowns, an herbalist crying his herbs and promising miraculous cures for all ills from sore throat to lovesickness, a carter with a load of timber, a countryman with a pig under his arm, a merchant in a long, fur-trimmed purple mantle, an archer with a crossbow: There was no end, it seemed, to the hustling crowd.

At the crossroads in the center of the city he was suddenly shoved against the wall as people pressed back to let a man have free passage. Adam stood on tiptoe to see who it was. He was running in the direction of the castle, and he wore a badge with the king's gold leopards and carried a spear. His face, Adam could see, was set and strained and he lifted his feet as if they were heavy. The crowd closed in behind him, and Adam had room to move again.

"Who was that?" he asked curiously of a student who was beside him.

"King's messenger," answered the young man carelessly. "He does better with his feet than most of us poor scholars will ever do with our heads. He gets threepence a day on the road and an allowance for shoes besides."

"I bet he needs the shoes," said Adam feelingly. "What was his message about, do you suppose?"

The scholar shrugged. "How should I know?"

"Do you think the fighting is over in Wales?"

The scholar had gone and he got no answer.

He found someone else to ask where Merton College was. The parson at Ewelme had got Perkin a place there as one of the incorporated scholars.

"Go past All Saints' Church, and past St. Mary's — that's the second one — and turn down the lane to the right till you come almost to the city wall."

It was a fine place, he thought when he saw it, Perkin had come to live and study in. There were several buildings, a smallish one with a steep stone roof, a long, low one, a half-finished chapel with scaffolding over it, a kitchen, if Adam's nose was any judge, and a hall with a great oak door all banded and barred with fine iron work.

While he stood there, shivering in the shadows gone suddenly chilly, the hall door swung open and he had a glimpse of long tables inside and people moving about in candlelight. Still holding Nick on the shortened leash, he climbed the stone steps and asked the first person he met for Perkin Watson.

The boy turned and bellowed into the long room, "Perkin!"

Perkin was new at Merton, and young besides, but he was not shy.

He hailed Adam with joy, admired his new clothes, patted Nick, and dragged them into the hall, announcing loudly, "Here's a minstrel!"

Some went on with what they were doing, one or two lifted an eyebrow as they went on, but several gathered around Adam.

"How good are you?" asked one flatly.

"Listen, and you can judge for yourself," answered Adam promptly.

He sang the Cuckoo Song, and they listened. He sang his own song about being a minstrel, and two more added themselves to the circle. When he sang "My love is to the greenwood gone," they joined in, and finally they all broke into "Gaudeamus igitur" and drowned Adam out.

The lusty song that students were singing all over Europe, urging one another to rejoice while they were young, for after youth and after age comes the grave, swelled out and filled the hall, and died away. Before a new song could be started, one of the scholars, who was older than the rest, jumped off the table where he had been perching, and said to Adam, "You've got a rare voice. Stay and have some supper with us."

"He's one of the seniors who govern the college," Perkin whispered.

Supper came in before long, and Adam was glad. It was preceded and followed by a long Latin grace rattled off by one of the scholars so fast that Adam could not separate one word from another. "That was pretty good time," Perkin told him. "They try to see who can do it the fastest."

Adam shared his supper with Nick, handing bits down under the table to him from time to time.

The talk at the table was all of the king's messenger.

"The king has called a Parliament at Westminster," said the senior whom Adam thought of as his friend.

"Is that all?" commented a round-faced boy, breaking his bread to dip it in his cup of ale.

Adam remembered the talk about parliaments in the Strangers' Hall at Winchester "Who goes to parliaments?" he said indignantly. "The big churchmen and the nobles! Do the common people go? They do not."

The senior pointed a long finger at him. "That's just where you're wrong, my young rooster," he said. "This one is different. For the first time the Commons *are* going to Parliament — two citizens or burgesses from every city and borough town. The Warden was with the Sheriff of Oxfordshire when the message came, and he saw it. "That which concerns all,' says King Edward, 'should be approved by all.' And that, my fellow scholars, if you could but see beyond the black letters in the books you bury your long noses in, is more important than any examinations you may or may not be passing."

His fellow scholars, whose noses were of varying length, united in a groan: "He's off again!"

Adam's mind went back to the old gaffer at Burford Bridge. What was it he had said about great things happening before people's eyes and they not seeing anything out of the ordinary? Perhaps the messenger that Adam had seen today was one like that. He sat dreaming till Perkin nudged him to go on with his meal.

After supper Perkin showed Adam over the college.

"Here's where we sleep," he said, when they came into the long, low building that Adam had noticed earlier. It was a big dormitory rather like the one at school, but with corners partitioned off to serve as studies. "That's my bed there. You can sleep with me tonight. Look out of the window."

Through the narrow window they saw the meadows beyond the city wall shining in the moonlight.

"See that tower over there, near the bridge?" said Perkin. "That's Friar Bacon's study."

"Who's he?" said Adam unimpressed.

"He's a very learned friar. Some say he's a magician. Friar Bacon says," went on Perkin, while they rested their elbows on the windowsill side by side and leaned out, "that there are four grounds of human ignorance. One is the placing of confidence in the opinion of the inexperienced — that is to say," he explained, bumping himself against Adam, "if I placed confidence in your opinion that would be a cause of my ignorance. And another is the hiding of one's lack of knowledge with a parade of super ficial wisdom — which might be a cause of *your* ignorance — " He stopped.

"And what," said Adam calmly, hooking his ankle suddenly around Perkin's and almost bringing him to the floor, "are the other two causes of human ignorance?"

"Those," said Perkin simply, "I have forgot."

"Ho!" cried Adam. "A scholar's life is easy! If a minstrel forgets he doesn't get any dinner."

"That gives me an idea," said Perkin "We'd better go to bed now, before anybody turns you out."

It was a tight squeeze in the narrow bed, and Adam was nervous anyhow, not being at all certain that the college authorities would want him to be there if they knew. When he did go to sleep he dreamed that the Warden came and with a thundering voice ordered the senior to throw him out of the window. He was relieved when morning came, and they rolled out early, before the other sleepers in the room were stirring.

"You know what?" said Perkin, while they were drawing water from the well to wash in. "I think you ought to stay here. There are some Poor Boys who aren't ready for the university yet that they keep here and teach, and when there's a vacancy among the scholars they move up the head Poor Boy. A scholar gets lodging and teaching and clothes and pocket money all the time he's studying. I should think they might take you. You've got more brains than half of these lumps. It wouldn't hurt to *ask*."

Adam remembered the Abbot's Steward at Watlington, and the message he had told Adam to give the Warden of Merton, but he shook his head.

"I don't want to be a clerk," he said. "I'm a minstrel. Listen!"

High overhead a bird went flying "Cuckoo!" it called. "Cuckoo!"

The first cuckoo! Now spring had really come! The quadrangle suddenly looked different. The grass seemed greener and the primroses beside the gate had burst into bloom during the night. Over the steep roof of the little Treasury building, a beech tree showed a tracery of tiny green leaves against the sky. Everything sparkled in the early sunshine, and the air smelled of spring.

"Cuckoo!" came the call again, more faintly.

"It's time for me to go to Ludlow," said Adam.

Perkin begged him to stay and go to the morning lecture with him, promising that afterward he would walk out beyond the north gate and say good-bye there. Adam agreed. He was sorry to leave Perkin; there was no one except Roger with whom he liked so much to be.

The lecture, which was all in Latin, was given in the hall. Adam was heartily sick of it long before it was finished. After all, he thought, squirming and sighing, he hadn't much time to spare.

He was still more impatient when, just as he and Perkin had got out into Merton Lane, a boy came running after them with a word that the Warden wanted to see them.

"Me?" said Perkin, turning pale.

"Both of you."

"Maybe," worried Adam, "I oughtn't to have stayed with you last night!"

At the best, it would mean delay; at the worst—he did not know what fearful academic penalties there might be. He was tempted to make a run for freedom, but he knew he could not leave Perkin to face alone whatever it might be.

They turned in silence and went back across the quadrangle to the Warden's lodging. "Come in," a voice answered their knock.

Adam opened the door. There were two men in the paneled room, but he saw only one.

"Roger!" he shouted.

Roger in his striped silk surcoat came striding toward him. Before the Warden and Perkin they merely shook hands, but in that instant Adam noticed that Roger had a fine pair of embroidered gloves and that he took off the right one to shake hands with Adam as if he had been a nobleman. Roger's hand was warm and strong, and Adam clung to it, too happy to speak.

"How did you know he was here?" burst out Perkin.

"I got to Ludlow earlier than I expected," replied Roger, "and the Steward of the Abbey of Bec was there holding court. He told me that he had met you, and that he had sent you to the Warden of Merton. So I came here to find you. The good Warden says the Abbot's Steward spoke well of you, Adam, and you may have a place here if you wish. Would you like that?"

"No, thank you," said Adam steadily. "I am a minstrel. I want to be on the road with you."

"I thought you would," said Roger. He went on talking, to give Adam time to recover from his surprise. "I gave Hugh the war horse, and he said to tell you he will lend him to you when you return. Simon is a knight now and has put away childish things. He sent you his silver flute, which is a fine thing for a young minstrel. Margery told me to be sure to bring you back to sing to her."

He looked down at Adam, who stood happy and sturdy and tall in his homemade blue and red, with his dog at his side and a bagpipe under his arm. Roger's mouth twitched at the corners, but his gray eyes deep under his square brow were tender.

"You have done well, son," he said.